Separation Anxiety

Separation Anxiety

Rohn Federbush

authorHOUSE®

AuthorHouse™
1663 Liberty Drive
Bloomington, IN 47403
www.authorhouse.com
Phone: 1 (800) 839-8640

Published by AuthorHouse 06/30/2015

ISBN: 978-1-5049-2012-4 (sc)
ISBN: 978-1-5049-2013-1 (e)

Print information available on the last page.

This book is printed on acid-free paper.

ACKNOWLEDGMENTS

My appreciation goes first to Paul Federbush for his loving, undaunted support. I value the time I stole to write, when I neglected my family and friends to create fictitious worlds. Also, as a voracious reader, I value my fellow writers in MMRWA, RWA, ACFW Great Lakes Chapter, RWAPro, and Ann Arbor City Club. I also wish to thank Elizabeth George and Northrup Frye for their continued inspiration and encouragement in this long, humbling voyage.

OTHER PUBLICATIONS

Salome's Conversion (2011)
1818, North Parish (2014)
1841, Floating Home (2014)
1879, Love's Triumph (2014)
Sally Bianco Mystery Series (2014)
Bonds of Affection (2014)

The final horror began the first week of the winter semester. Who knew three of Curtain Taylor's college friends would lose their lives to a serial killer within the year?

CHAPTER ONE

Wednesday, January 9
Seminar
Michigan Museum of Paleontology

Sitting next to Curtain Taylor in the back row of the first-floor auditorium, Ike St. Claire slid her cryptic note over Curtain's open laptop. Ike swept her long, black hair behind her shoulders, waiting for Curtain's response to her note.

Curtain whispered, "They're leaving for Chicago in May."

At the age of twenty-two, Nosey Petersen and Blacky Schultz, Curtain's older sorority sisters, had won assistant curator positions in Chicago's Field Museum of Natural History. They would be leaving at the end of the winter term, when they finished their undergraduate degrees in zoology.

Matt must have read the note from the row behind them, because he tapped her back and whispered, "Me too, Drape."

The girls had nicknamed her Drape four years earlier, when Curtain first entered the Sigma Kappa Sorority. Entering college at sixteen, Drape needed to fit in quickly with the older crowd. She actually loved the pun on her stupid moniker. Mother hated it, which added to the name's appeal. Her close-knit circle of friends all adopted nicknames to keep hers company.

Drape's stomach hurt, and she wasn't hungry. Who would keep the young girls safe in the big city? Matt North had only started shaving the week before Thanksgiving.

Drape bowed her head for a silent plea: *Lord, keep my friends free of all harm.* The familiar layout of tiered rows of narrow tables shifted for her. The winter sun reflected off of one student's metal pen, the laptop screens of several others, and the plastic back of someone's three-ring binder. Drape blinked, and her eyes watered. A deep sadness and cold fear crept into her heart, spreading across her chest and down her arms, until she placed her cold thumb on her bottom lip. She knew negative fears were not sent from God.

Now only Ike, Stone, and Sky would call her Drape. She would miss Nosey Peterson's bookish snobbery and Blacky Schultz's redheaded craziness. Of course, heart-struck Matt North would follow Blacky anywhere. Nosey was the one to blame, if you could fault someone for foresight and competitive drive. The two zoology graduates had landed their first assignments.

Chicago, the murder capital of the world, was too big. Drape could always find her sisters in Ann Arbor, but Chicago's acres of buildings and mammoth highway systems ruled out any hope of keeping in daily touch with Blacky and Nosey. One unanswered text and they could be lost forever.

Cosmos Henderson, known to Drape's friends as Sky, would understand her concern. He might even drive down from Brighton to be with her. That's what fiancés were supposed to do—provide comfort when needed, right? But Drape didn't want pity. She wanted everything to stay the same: to be sixteen again with Sky as the exciting, older teaching assistant in her advanced college calculus, with her four beautiful sorority sisters at the dinner table each night, and even with Matt tagging along every time they stepped outside.

"Does Stone know?" Drape whispered.

Ike shook her head. "She'll get all paranoid."

Drape pushed her iPad into her backpack. No sense trying to listen to Professor Leland's lecture on the history of the museum when her mind couldn't absorb one syllable.

"I know where Stone is." Drape slid out of her seat and headed for the back exit of the lecture hall. Matt North and Ike St. Claire followed.

In the hall, Drape scowled at them. "Hey, you guys. Someone needs to stay. I'll need Professor Leland's lecture notes."

Matt unwound his maize-and-blue scarf and shuffled back to the auditorium's door. "Tell Stone I'll take care of the girls."

Ike tapped Drape's shoulder. "Stone won't believe Matt can save himself, much less manage metropolitan terrors."

"You think it's dangerous too?"

Behind Drape, Ike stopped her climb up the marble staircase for a moment. "Neither of them have family in Chicago. All of Blacky's family is in Florida like yours."

Drape turned around to ask, "Does Nosey have family?"

"I think she was hatched."

In the zoology museum's second-floor specimen-cleaning lab, they found Stone Slager watching the dermestid beetles. The bugs were scrubbing the flesh and connective tissue off a freshly skinned, dried, and resoaked red fox carcass from South America, the *Vulpes vulpes.*

Stone wiped her nose and pushed up her horn-rimmed glasses. "Why are you two not at the seminar?"

"Listen, Mother Stone." Ike batted Stone's clipboard. "Nosey, Blacky, and Matt are leaving in May. They won those jobs in Chicago."

"Matt?" Stone asked. "He didn't apply or interview in Chicago."

Drape could give her that. "He's not going to be separated from Blacky."

"Like Sky left you." Stone sniffed.

"Sky's only twenty minutes away, Stone." Drape took off her own gold-trimmed glasses. Stone didn't look dignified in her studious frames, just slightly stupid with all the sniffing and snuffling. Maybe laser eye surgery would help Drape. She could use clear lenses in designer frames for intellectual acceptance. Drape also made a mental note to ask Professor Hazzard to install a vent over the waist-high feeding box to cut down on any noxious fumes.

"How can they leave Ann Arbor?" Stone shifted her stance.

Drape didn't want to leave Ann Arbor either. Both Ike and Stone were interviewing for jobs at the university. Ann Arbor's slower pace, sylvan riverside parks, rich live entertainment venues, artsy book culture, myriad coffee shops, and trendy restaurants were all difficult to imagine giving up.

On Christmas Eve, when Drape had been in the holiday spirit, generous and glowing from Sky's touching proposal, she'd agreed to marry him even though she was only eighteen. Around Sky she was a normal female searching for a suitable mate. He exuded a warmth that spread through her body down to her toes. Her gratitude to him for actually wanting her right back made her lightheaded at times.

Drape had immediately set about finding a decent place to live in Brighton for after the wedding. Sky had started his Lansing mathematics professorship in January, so Grandma had purchased the condo for them. Situated halfway between the two cities, the twenty-minute drive from Brighton to either Ann Arbor or Lansing would be doable for each of them.

Ike spun on her heels. "We need to give our sorority sisters a great send-off."

"Not until May," Drape said, not wanting to think about losing them. "I need to call Sky."

"Any excuse to see your lover boy." Ike huffed.

"My fiancé." Drape tried to come up with a plausible pretext for phoning Sky. "He might have friends who can help the girls in Chicago." Mostly, she wanted to lay hands on him, to make sure he was there for her, and to feel his heartbeat race when she stayed close too long.

Stone wiped her dry forehead with the back of her hand. "My mother knows a retired policeman who works as a guard at The Field Museum. Nosey met him during summer break. Too young for Mother. He's Italian, about forty, with beautiful white hair. He's perfectly capable of protecting Nosey and Blacky."

"Why would he be interested?" Ike asked.

Stone laughed. "Oh, Salvatore Bianco will be interested. I told you, he's Italian. He owns an apartment close to the museum. Nosey saw the place when she visited us. Mother's in Evanston now. We were able to put up a two-story Christmas tree because of the balcony bedroom. You know, it hangs over the kitchen, so the front room's ceiling is real high." Stone lifted her arms and then dropped them when no one seemed impressed. "Farther north is quieter too."

Ike turned away. "Anyone ever tell you your stories have no point?"

"They do." Drape winked at Ike. "I want to know Blacky and Nosey will be safe. You've heard about all those murders in Chicago."

"Murder capital of the world," Ike said. "A godless place."

"The Lord's kingdom is everywhere." Drape sent another plea to the Lord: *Please set a hedge of spiritual safety around my friends.*

Drape reviewed her King James daily, underlined passages in red, and posted them to her Facebook page. She usually skipped the didactic sermons because she felt that once the Lord arrived in heaven, He realized His sacrifice freed all sinners after their deaths. And the loving certitudes were easier for nonbelievers to swallow.

It wasn't as if Drape avoided advice. Recently she'd been carefully rereading Proverbs. Apropos for the day's worries, Proverbs 1:7 said, "The fear of the Lord is the beginning of knowledge, but fools despise wisdom and instruction."

* * *

Thursday, January 10
Brighton Condo

Sky had to laugh at Drape inviting Ike and Stone along as chaperones. You'd think she'd know he'd honor her wishes to wait until the marriage night. But no, now he had to stretch his spaghetti-and-meatball dinner to include them. He couldn't recall if either Ike or Stone were vegetarians, which would help with the meatball distribution.

"Just a few more minutes," Sky called into the family room as he broke apart the rest of the lettuce to fill out the salad. Drape should have called ahead at least. Then he remembered two hard-boiled eggs intended for his lunch and diced them for a topping. He rinsed off a can of anchovies meant for pizza and chopped them up; then he tossed the salad for perfect distribution. The loaf of Italian bread wouldn't provide any leftovers, but that was okay.

"Smells good." Ike craned her neck over the breakfast island. "Stone won't eat those meatballs."

Sky winked at the tall, almond-eyed beauty, and whispered, "More for us."

Drape was setting the table with Stone's help, if rolling napkins could count as help. Drape entered the kitchen and untied Sky's apron. "We need to figure out how to keep Nosey and Blacky protected while they're in Chicago."

"Matt's worthless," Stone said. "I'll call Mother again tonight to find out if Salvatore has any vacant apartments in his building."

Sky stole a swift kiss from Drape. It was warming, even if their touch was only for a second. Her hazel eyes stayed tender as he ladled the sauce without the meatballs into the bowl she was holding. "Matt's not a bad kid."

"Still, as you say, merely a boy." Drape nudged his shoulder as she passed him to serve the spaghetti sauce.

Ike laughed. "I don't think we can count on Matt growing inches or muscles by May."

"Sky," Stone said, "thanks for including us. You're a great cook."

"All of you are always welcome." Sky set the giant bowl of spaghetti next to Stone, moving the tongs to her side of the bowl. "Help yourself. Why didn't you bring Nosey and Blacky with you?"

"Matt would have come too," Ike said, counting the meatballs and taking her share.

Sky smiled as he assessed the position of Drape's friends in their life together. Stone wasn't exactly a sociable person, dressing without apparent thought. Tonight an orange sweater hung loosely over green stretch Levis. Ike, dressed totally in black, was always stunning, but Drape often criticized her unthinking callousness, like when she told Matt he was too short for her. Blacky always had plans to enjoy some event, and Nosey kept Drape abreast of the newest books and magazine articles to read. Drape's entertainment committee would diminish soon. Losing Nosey and Blacky to Chicago's mayhem might leave Drape lonesome enough to set a wedding date in the near future. He smiled at his lady across the table. Her yellow cashmere sweater was out of his reach. He wanted to hold her chin, get his fill of gazing into her eyes, and tuck her flyaway brown hair behind her ears so he could nibble her earlobe. She seemed to like that, having gone limp in his arms the last time.

Sky focused on his plate. He couldn't push her for a wedding date, not in front of her buddies. Surely Drape knew he wanted her to join him in their condo—actually her condo—as his wife. Drape had insisted his name go on the deed, but the money was Mother Taylor's or maybe her grandmother's. He hadn't met her Seattle family in the four years he'd known Drape. They'd moved to Florida as soon as she finished her first semester. Drape wasn't the needy type, but she was less confident after she lost any chance at a future homecoming to the place that was no longer her home.

Sky pushed his remaining meatball around his plate. Drape was staring at him. "One meatball," he sang. "Remember that old jazz song from the Depression era?"

"I do," Drape said, "but I can't remember the name of the performer.

"You'll remember on the ride home," Ike said.

Drape smiled at Sky. "I'm going to miss the girls. Stone knows a guard at the museum who owns an apartment building close by it. He might have an opening for them. Salvatore Bianco is forty, right?"

Stone nodded, intent on twisting her last bit of spaghetti onto her fork.

"How does your mother know this Salvatore Bianco?" Sky shifted in his chair.

Stone finished a mouthful before answering. "Her landlord, I think. But she's moved to a bigger apartment, farther north on the lakefront."

* * *

Drape wished she had come alone. Sky was so manly and cute at the same time, cooking up a storm and making the meal stretch for them. It would be nice to come home from Ann Arbor to dinner already on the table. Of course Sky would be working in Lansing, so they would share the cooking. He'd hardly eaten because he was too busy staring at her. She wanted to start their married life, make babies with a real man, not follow her mother's solution of getting a sperm-bank father. Sky accepted the empty side of her family tree more easily than Drape did. Would she be a good parent without knowing how a normal family raised a child?

Interrupting a conversation between Ike and Stone about Blacky's scattered and dyslexic brain waves, Drape announced, "Sky wants me to set a wedding date. Do you think Nosey and Blacky would come back to be my bridesmaids?"

Ike looked at Stone. "What are we, chopped liver?"

"No, no," Drape laughed. "I want you both. Ike, would you be my maid of honor?"

Stone pointed to her chest and laughed. "Guess who's chopped liver now?"

"When?" Sky wanted to know, tugging at the back of his hair. Did the pain help him remember not to let tears materialize?

"Saturday, June fifteenth. Okay?" Drape asked.

Sky flew at her, nearly knocking her off her chair with his embrace. He knelt down. "I was hoping," he said. "I was hoping."

* * *

7

Saturday, January 12
Sigma Kappa House

Their sorority-house mother, Mrs. Mack, laid a fine spread in her small dining room. Linens, flowers, the best Haviland china, crystal, a full complement of utensils, and candlelight all taught Mrs. Mack's live-in charges about the elegant touches of fine dining. The rest of the sorority residents ate in the cafeteria at odd hours.

For Drape, the meatloaf smells triggered childish fears of being in danger without a male in the house to protect her and her mother. Drape missed her grandmother. Somehow the morning's Proverb (1:17) had unsettled her with its warning: "Surely in vain the net is spread in the sight of any bird." She drew her chair up to the table and announced Ike would be her maid of honor.

Blacky Schultz ignored the red curls escaping from her upswept style and claimed her role in the wedding plans. "I'll do the shower. What's a good date? We should invite both Sky's parents and yours, because then Matt and his father will feel welcome. Matt will arrange the wedding's limo service."

Drape hadn't told her mother or grandma she'd set a date yet. "Florida's pretty far to come for a shower and then return for the wedding."

"Nonsense," Mrs. Mack said. "We'll make room for them here. Most of the girls won't be around. When is the shower?"

Nosey Peterson said, "May eleventh is a Saturday. Won't your parents be here for Commencement anyway?"

"They're planning to stay at the Michigan League's hotel, Mrs. Mack. Mother and Grandma are yearly donors to the trust. I need to call them with the wedding date."

"Good," Blacky said. "I'll send out the shower invitations the first of April."

Ike suppressed a giggle. "If you don't tell your folks, Drape, they'll think it's an April Fool's joke."

Nosey shook her head in disapproval. "I'll call Pastor Nieman to line up St. Andrew's for the service."

"He'll want to counsel the couple," Mrs. Mack said.

"Sky's not a believer." Under the tabletop, Drape picked at her napkin's embroidered sorority emblem.

Nosey cocked her head. "You still believe God is interested in you? I can swallow the Creator of the Universe bit, but not the day-by-day personal attention."

"Why do you attend St. Andrew's if you don't believe in our Savior?" Drape asked.

"She's hedging her bets," Ike said.

"Isn't there something in the Bible about not being unequally yoked?" Stone took another bite of her dessert.

Blacky raised her water glass in Stone's direction. "How about Mark 9:41? About giving a cup of water to a believer? Sky's planning to do more than that."

Drape spoke with a certainty she didn't feel. "Sky will want Pastor Nieman to marry us at St. Andrew's. It is a historic and beautiful Gothic church." He'd better.

Stone scratched under her tangled brown hair. Mrs. Mack frowned in Stone's direction. However, nonverbal censure was wasted on Stone, who was oblivious to nearly all social cues.

Drape decided her wedding dress would include enough silk petticoats to mimic the hooped-skirts of the Civil War era, when St. Andrew's was constructed.

Stone seemed to wake up and finally notice she hadn't volunteered for wedding duty. "Ike, would you go with me to order the wedding invitations and flowers?"

Ike brushed her long, dark hair behind her shoulder. "Doesn't Drape need to pick out the flowers she wants? Are we going to *drape* all those pews in St. Andrew's?" Ike muffled a laugh. "Drape, Drape's flowers, get it?"

If she joined the laughter, Drape felt she'd dissolve into hysterics. "When am I going to have time to get all this done? My PhD thesis defense, shopping for a wedding dress, entertaining Mother and Grandma when they arrive ... Maybe I should set a later date."

"No!" Everyone in the room shouted.

Then she did laugh. "Okay, okay. I'll just be a paragon of efficiency."

* * *

Sunday, January 13
Zoology Museum

After attending eight o'clock mass at St. Andrew's by herself, Drape plugged in her laptop and began tallying bone measurements of the 2010 grey fox, *Lycalopex griseus*, specimen. Concentrating on her thesis, investigating how species adapted to climate changes in their development history, relaxed her turbulent thoughts. Drape had read Proverbs 1:11 to reflect on during the day: "How long, ye simple ones, will you love simplicity? And the scorners delight in their scorning, and the fools hate knowledge?"

Perhaps the Lord wanted her to uncover evidence of global warming along with the species variables. Wedding plans were shelved on her cell phone's calendar.

An hour later Professor Jane Hazzard knocked on the table to get Drape's attention. "You're really focused. I have a minute or two. Should we set up your committee and schedule your defense before graduation?"

"Absolutely." Drape switched files on her screen. Professor Hazzard still wore her lab coat, meaning even on Sunday a minute or two was really all the time she could spare. "Is Friday, March fifteenth free on your calendar?"

Professor Hazzard consulted her cell phone. "Two o'clock, at Rackham or in the Museum?"

"The Museum," Drape decided. "Easier to assemble everyone."

Professor Hazzard nodded. "You'll need statisticians to convince Leland, Foster, and Carrington that weather and foraging variations caused significant changes in the skulls. They'll be skeptical enough of an eighteen-year-old gaining a doctoral degree."

Drape recognized her age was a factor in convincing others she was capable. She typed the names onto the Rackham Committee form: Professor Jake Carrington, Mammal Division Collections Curator; Professor Carl Foster, Museum Director; Professor Ray Lelend, Museum Historian. Then she said, "My fiancé graduated from the Department of Mathematics two years ago. He's still friends with Professors Roy Clarke and Paul Chinich. Will they do?"

"Perfect. Obtain their signatures of permission, and nail down the defense date. Give me a month to read your thesis before you submit the final to them." Professor Hazzard turned to leave.

Drape resumed her solitary laboratory chores and was startled when someone touched her shoulder.

Professor Hazzard had returned. "When you're substitute teaching in Professor Pollack's calculus class, remember to take your time explaining the terms to the female students. We're newbies in this male-dominated field. Promise?"

"I will." Drape wondered if Professor Hazzard had faced more obstacles than she'd encountered herself. Perhaps the world was changing faster than Professor Hazzard realized. Drape touched her forehead. Had her skull grown to accommodate more brain cells because opportunities had opened up for women in the last few decades? Was she like a well-fed red fox eating restaurant garbage in Patagonia?

She switched on her phone, saving the February 15 deadline to her crowded calendar. There was less than a month to collect her data and come up with plausible conclusions. She certainly didn't have time to plan a wedding.

Please, Lord, she prayed, *grant me victory over my present difficulties so that I might bear witness to those I'm trying to help of your power, your love, and your glory.*

Restored to calm, Drape's mind switched back to the final measurements she would make before comparing her results to fifty samples from each of the ten fox species in the Western Hemisphere.

* * *

Sigma Kappa Sorority

Later that night, Mrs. Mack knocked on Drape's bedroom door. "No. You will not work through dinner. Your friends need to see a balanced leader, able to work and socialize."

"Yes, ma'am." Drape saved her work on the computer and checked her appearance in the full-length mirror on the back of her door before pulling on an extra sweater and following her sorority mother to the dining room. Food would recharge her brain, and the girls needed her wedding input.

Mrs. Mack, who always sat at the head of the table, had changed the place cards again, making sure Stone was seated next to a different sorority sister each evening to improve her table manners by example. Tonight Stone sat on Drape's left.

As soon as Drape was seated, Stone started the conversation. "Lilies of the Valley are all fine and good for your bouquet, Drape, but they will not serve well as garlands for the pews."

From across the table, Ike handed Drape three sample invitation cards. "I like the solid white, but the embossed cream design is elegant, and then there's this campy rainbow one for the shower, Blacky."

"Cream for the wedding and white for the shower," Drape said. "Use both my mother and my grandmother's names. Couldn't we use evergreens, Mrs. Mack, and poke a few lilies into the top at each pew?"

Mrs. Mack smiled and passed Stone a dish of mashed potatoes.

Stone helped herself while Mrs. Mack held the dish. Then Stone said to Drape, "Who is going to walk you down the aisle?" Stone held onto the serving spoon. "The expense to ship all those ..."

Taking the dish from Mrs. Mack and passing it to Blacky, Ike laughed. "Stone, we're not working on the cheap. The sky's the limit, right, Drape?"

Drape shook her head. "You know, Ike, your puns are sometimes labored."

"But not your budget?" Ike glared at Stone. "Stone, pass Mrs. Mack the serving spoon."

Drape said. "I'm only going to do this once."

"That's what they all say," Nosey blurted.

Mrs. Mack frowned. "A marriage commitment does not guarantee every day will be trouble free. Life happens. But the emotional bond will see you through to the next good day. Commitments are similar to integrity. You either have it or you don't. There is no middle ground."

The girls were ready to bolt away from another tutelage session, so Drape said, "I really appreciate your work and the time you're taking away from your studies."

Blacky interrupted. "Stone, you said we could talk to your police detective."

"Retired, policeman," Stone said. "I'll conference call him, if Mrs. Mack permits it."

"After dessert, Stone." Mrs. Mack glanced at the separate plates of custard pie waiting on the sideboard for her beleaguered crew. "No one is injured or about to board an airplane, so we *will* finish our meal."

Maybe the other girls found Mrs. Mack tiresome, but not Drape. Drape had imprinted all of the older woman's dictates as goals to incorporate into her future family's life. Drape's upbringing encompassed few family meals, just holidays when non-Chinese restaurants were unavailable. Even then, Grandma was the one who cooked the turkey and set the dining room table, not Drape's mother.

Drape counted her friends. Matt and Sky were not present, but Blacky, Nosey, Stone, and Ike composed a reasonable number of children for a family. One to hold each hand for her and Sky. She could see them walking together in a grassy park, the two girls with her, the baby boys swinging Sky's arms. "Perfect."

"Thank you," Mrs. Mack said, erroneously thinking she'd been paid a compliment for the pie.

Ike cocked an eyebrow in Drape's direction. "Mrs. Mack, may we stay at the table to listen to this landlord?"

"Of course, Ike." Mrs. Mack brushed nonexistent crumbs off her skirt. "Stone, do call. We'll use the speaker phone."

After Stone pulled the phone to the center of the table, she punched in the landlord's number.

"Salvatore Bianco," a low male voice answered.

"It's Stone, Salvatore. You're on the speaker phone. My sorority sisters wanted to talk to you before we entrust Blacky and Nosey to your care."

"Hello, Nosey. I remember showing you the Field's zoology collections. Be glad to answer any questions about the apartments or the walk to the museum. It's four blocks away and well-lit at night."

"Are there neighborhood bars?" Ike asked.

"No," Salvatore laughed. "Coffee shops for all those intellectuals. I think they drink alone, at home."

"I like your laugh," Drape said and then blushed. She shrugged her shoulders at Nosey. "It sounds genuine."

Ike made a face at Drape, who realized she was reacting weirdly.

Blacky asked, "Do the apartments face Lake Michigan?"

13

"Sorry," Salvatore said. "There's a park between the museum and the lake. The trees are bare now, but there are cherry and apple blossoms in the spring. And the maples are great in the fall."

Nosey spoke up next. "When I visited with Stone last summer, someone mentioned live theatre quite close to Lake Michigan?"

"In the park," Salvatore said. "You'll find the Goodman schedule on the web. Stone's mother said I should visit Ann Arbor to let your families get to know me."

Ike pounded the table. "We weren't born here. Our parents live in Illinois, Indiana, and Florida, respectively."

Stone twirled her dark hair then used her napkin to wipe her nose.

Mrs. Mack tsk'd at her. "Please do visit, Mr. Bianco. Nosey and Stone have already given us a good report of your ability to watch over the girls. We'll be happy to meet with you. Their schedules are rather busy."

"I'll make train reservations," Salvatore said. "Pick a day. You can all come take a look at the place. I'll arrange tickets to a Goodman play."

"After my defense, March fifteenth," Drape suggested.

"*Measure for Measure*, it is," Salvatore said. "I'll come out there on March twenty-second and take you all back with me. You'll be home by noon on Sunday."

Stone raised one thick eyebrow. "Drape, that will be seven tickets to pay for?"

"Yes," Drape said. "And, I'll feel better knowing where to find Blacky and Nosey, when I want them."

Ike shook her head. "Have you ever examined your control issues?"

Salvatore interrupted. "The end of March is a good time to visit my apartment building. Students will be moving out for the end of the term and you'll be able to pick out the best choices. They are fully furnished."

Blacky wrinkled her nose. "We'll be able to replace the furniture with our own, won't we?"

"Of course," Salvatore said. "Can't wait to meet you all. Stone, I'll phone your mother."

Nosey and Stone both acted surprised.

"Well okay," Stone said. "Thanks, Salvatore. Bye."

Mrs. Mack broke the silence. "Stone, I think you should be congratulated for resolving your friends' relocation issues."

"I hope so." Stone said it like she'd failed to ask Salvatore a question. "Drape, could Salvatore walk you down the aisle? I mean, if you like him?"

"Sorry, Stone," Drape apologized. "He does sound gentlemanly, but Sky mentioned Professor Clarke asked to do the honors, when he told him about the sperm bank."

"Drape," Mrs. Mack interjected. "I think we can come up with a more sociably acceptable way of acknowledging your father's absence from your wedding."

Ike looked ticked off. "There is no way to put a spin on a sperm bank!"

"No name for the invitation," Stone said quietly.

Blacky started a sentence, "More importantly ..."

Nosey finished the thought, raising her voice up a notch in volume: "No father in the home!"

Loyalty from friends was a blessing. As was her habit, Drape sent a prayer off to the Lord when she felt uncomfortable with Mother's unusual approach to motherhood. *Lord, Thy will be done, and forgive my trespasses as I forgive those who trespass against me.*

The familiar prayer reminded her of the wasted hours spent in therapy, trying to find a way to present the facts surrounding her birth to acquaintances and how to fill out forms asking for both parents' names. She had no explanation, no excuses, and really no understanding of the trauma her mother endured as a childless woman.

Mother had referred her to the Bible story about Hannah who had no children even though she was well loved by her husband. The Old Testament woman was ridiculed by the second wife who had produced ten male children. So Hannah prayed for a child, promising to give him to the Lord's service. After she weaned her only son, she presented him to the temple. Hannah gifted her only son back to the Lord to claim motherhood.

At least Mother had kept her, not given her to a nunnery or to some stranger to raise. But Drape wanted to mother a full house with a husband included in the deal. Together they would bring up their children to the best of their combined abilities.

Sky understood. He had reassured her more than once. "You'll be a great mother. You're so gentle with my failings. You don't have a trace of a temper. We'll work together to give our children a stable home with two loving parents."

Drape did thank the Lord daily for her abilities, her health, and the love of her mother, grandmother, and Sky. All she really desired in life was to create a family of her own, under the Lord's guidance.

CHAPTER TWO

Monday, January 14
Zingerman's Roadhouse Restaurant

Sky's palms were damp. He was never comfortable asking friends for favors, but Drape might need his help to convince his old math professors to serve on her defense committee.

When he arrived at the Roadhouse, Professor Clarke's smile eased Sky's concerns. The man did everything possible to facilitate graduate students' progress.

They both reached for Professor Chinich's coat as he stormed into the crowded foyer, shedding a different-colored hat, gloves, and scarf in a flurry of swinging arms. "Am I late? The traffic has not improved even with the new bridge."

"My fiancée hasn't arrived yet," Sky explained. "The hostess says we need to wait ten minutes to be seated."

"No reservations?" Chinich asked.

"With reservations," Sky said. His ears were tingling so he knew they were turning red with embarrassment.

"Sky?" Drape pulled on the back of his cardigan.

He wanted to embrace her. She was such a fresh contrast of youthful beauty to these wizened old friends. But instead he reached for both of her gloved hands, desperate for touch in the crowded entryway. "Drape." It was all he could say. Coughing to hide the onslaught of emotions, he said slowly, "Ten minute wait."

"Professors," Drape said. "Thank you for coming. Do you like Zingerman's?"

"I do," Professor Clarke said.

"Expensive for the quality," Chinich said loudly enough for the hostess to hear.

The maître d motioned to Sky, who thought she might ask them to leave the restaurant. "I have your table ready. Follow me." She pointed to a booth at the back of the room.

"This is fine," Drape said. "Sit next to me, Sky."

She could pump up his confidence so easily. Did every future bridegroom feel as elated with his fiancée's presence? Sky didn't know, but he smiled at both professors. This delicate splendor seated next to him would soon be his wife.

Professor Clarke slid into the booth opposite Drape.

Chinich dithered, looking about the room perhaps considering another seating arrangement. "Don't know a soul," he said, apparently disappointed at his lack of notoriety.

"Let me introduce myself." Professor Clarke laughed.

Chinich grinned. "Oh, you! I guess you three will have to do."

Once they ordered—which took a considerable amount of time, since the waitress had to convince Professor Chinich the soup was entirely vegetarian and contained no wine, even after checking with the cook twice—Sky relaxed.

Drape carried the evening's conversation, concentrating on Chinich's life history: his beginnings at Rutgers, MIT, a stint at Princeton, and then retiring from MIT as a physicist to become a mathematician at the University of Michigan.

Then she asked them both, "Will Fourier's shape analysis adequately represent changes in skull dimensions to convince zoology professors my thesis is correct?"

Chinich jumped in. "Well, it would be your job to be specific enough about the accuracy and or errors of your technique."

"I believe the encroachment of civilization and the resultant changes to the eating habits of fox in the Western Hemisphere can be documented. I've measured the skull size of *Zorro* specimens, the Artic Fox, the Cape Fox, the Crab-eating Fox, the Sechura Desert Fox, the Bengal Fox, the Swift Fox and specifically compared the Patagonia Red Fox to the Illinois Red Fox."

"A problem can be treated quite statistically," Sky offered. He left his sandwich on his plate.

Drape wasn't eating, either. "The examples span 1860 to 2010. What is the most common error in data collection? I'm able to compare fifty-year separations in specimens from the same location with scattered weather variations and infringements by human developers during the sample periods."

"Of course," Professor Clarke said. "You'll compare your research techniques to some similar problems well-studied in the literature to see how well they agree."

Drape fiddled with her engagement ring before asking, "What percentage of change would be significant?"

Chinich motioned for the waitress to take his soup bowl away. "There's no general answer."

Professor Clarke reached across the table and patted Drape's hand. "How much do skulls of foxes vary interspecifically?"

"I have looked into those studies on the specimens I am measuring." Drape said. "Even interspecifically, notable changes in length to width, tooth wear, eye socket shapes, and ear aperture shapes occur throughout the decades where there is significant climate change, perhaps due to intrusions of human civilization."

"I'd be interested to see your results," Professor Clarke said, poking Chinich's side.

"What? Oh," Chinich said. "When is your defense scheduled, again?"

Sky took the first bite of his Reuben. The aromas of sauerkraut and corned beef matched the flavors. All was well with his world and Drape's.

* * *

Tuesday, January 15
Sigma Kappa House

At breakfast, Drape went over the calendar on her phone. Mrs. Mack banned telephone conversations at table. "Mrs. Mack?" Drape slipped the offending device into her backpack. "You wouldn't happen to know where I could purchase one of those large paper calendars like the one Grandma kept on her writing desk to record my middle–school gymnast meets and exam schedules?"

Blacky was sitting on Drape's right. "Mrs. Mack, there's one hanging in the foyer, but no one's written on it."

Mrs. Mack passed Stone more fragrant bacon. They were all accustomed to the fact that Stone wouldn't remember to pass the dish. Waiting patiently until Stone had selected a sufficient amount, Mrs. Mack then offered the platter to Blacky. "Help yourself to the calendar, Drape. I thought you all might want to write down your class schedules for me."

Ike and Nosey rolled their eyes at each other.

"Thank you, Mrs. Mack," Drape said. "It will help keep me on track with all these dates floating around in my head."

Always the tease, Ike asked, "Schedule rather full, is it?"

Drape didn't catch on. Grandma and Mother were serious people. "Wedding Saturday, June fifteenth, shower Saturday, May eleventh, defense Friday, March fifteenth, and final thesis to Professor Hazzard Friday, February fifteenth."

Stone's sense of humor was nonexistent. "Don't forget exams, Thursday, April twenty-fifth through Friday, May second; and Commencement, Sunday, May fifth."

"When do your mother and grandmother arrive?" Nosey asked, winking at Ike.

"Saturday, May fourth," Drape said.

"Heavens!" Ike jumped up in mock horror. "There aren't enough days left to choose a wedding cake, buy a dress, and decorate the church. Life is too complicated to live!"

"Give it a break." Drape dug into her buttered cinnamon roll. "I get the picture." The morning's scripture, Proverbs 1:33 echoed, "But whoso hearkenth unto me shall dwell safely, and be quiet from fear or evil."

"Sufficient unto the day," Stone said, not really understanding the joke on Drape. "Don't forget Salvatore will be here Friday, March twenty-second, to take us to Chicago."

"Sky wants to meet him," Drape said.

"So does Matt," Blacky said.

"Isn't Matt moving into the same apartment building?" Mrs. Mack asked.

"It's only for women," Nosey answered.

"Matt will search for his own place the weekend of the play." Blacky pulled at a loose curl. "He says he has references for another limo job in

Chicago. I worry he won't be safe, driving all those gangsters around late at night."

Stone reached for more bacon. "Instead of worrying, I just pray. Did I tell you all, I haven't heard from Mother. I have left her telephone messages, texts and emails. I can't imagine where she'd go this long without telling me."

"She doesn't know you are introducing Blacky and Matt to Salvatore?" Nosey asked.

"Not yet," Stone said.

Drape felt a chill enter the room. She looked behind her to the open dining room door, half expecting Matt or Sky to have entered the house, but no one was there. *Lord,* she prayed, *keep us all safely in Your arms.*

"Amen," Stone said out loud, her head bowed, obviously ending a prayer of her own.

A firm believer in the Lord's powers, Mrs. Mack took a more practical approach to life's mysteries. "Stone, how long has it been since you talked to your mother?"

"I was with her for Christmas in Evanston." Stone stood, keeping her hands on the back of her chair. "I came back on the second."

Drape cocked her head. She didn't see a problem. "Mother and Grandma haven't spoken to me since the Christmas break either."

"You just saw them," Ike said. "What's the big deal?"

Mrs. Mack wouldn't let it go. "Drape, you haven't told them about your wedding date or the shower, but Stone's been trying to reach her mother. Since when, Stone?"

Stone was scratching behind her ears, but Mrs. Mack didn't frown at her. "The day I mentioned Salvatore, didn't I?"

Ike answered for them. "January tenth, Thursday, when you went with Drape and me to Sky's in Brighton."

"So you called Salvatore Bianco, without speaking to your mother." Nosey looked at Blacky.

"When he talked to all of us, he said he'd spoken to your mother," Drape said.

"No," Stone said. "He said he would call her. I wondered if he would reach her, but I didn't want to admit to you all that Mother hadn't returned my calls yet."

They all knew Stone's mother seemed estranged. They had chalked it up to Stone's lack of sociability caused by a mild autism on the intelligent end of the Asperger's scale.

Mrs. Mack excused herself. "Blacky, would you pour everyone another cup of coffee? I want to make a phone call to see if we can clear this up."

Blacky cheerfully refilled their breakfast coffee cups.

Drape's stomach wasn't sure coffee was a good idea, so she finished off her orange juice, cinnamon roll and glass of milk before Mrs. Mack returned.

"I'm glad you all waited." Mrs. Mack sat back down and Blacky removed her coffee cup and replaced it with a hotter one. "Larry Combs is an old friend of mine. He's a private detective and has agreed to go to Chicago for you, Stone. He'll check out Salvatore Bianco too."

Stone sat back down, rescuing her napkin from her chair and then using it to blow her nose.

Mrs. Mack's eyebrows went up, but she didn't make a remark. "I gave Larry your mother's address in Evanston and he'll call me as soon as he arrives. Now you all go about your schedules. I'll call your cell phone, Stone, as soon as I hear anything."

Blacky brought up the shower plans. "Drape, tell me when you've telephoned *your* mother." She asked Mrs. Mack, "I'm assuming we can hold the shower here?"

"Yes, yes," Mrs. Mack said. "I'm looking forward to it. We've held fifteen showers in this house for your sorority sisters over the years. I think we should invite them too. Just to keep in touch with our happenings. I doubt many will show up."

Drape was shocked. "Mrs. Mack, please don't. Blacky and Nosey are relocating and need their resources to furnish their rooms."

"Oh, Sigma Kappa will finance the shower, Blacky." Mrs. Mack straightened her pearls. "I thought you all understood that when I mentioned inviting the sorority."

"How many do you expect?" Drape asked.

"Well," Mrs. Mack demurred. "That depends on their health and the weather. There are about thirty who keep in touch regularly— Christmas letters. I've gotten quite close over the years with my family." She smiled at each of them.

Drape understood. They were all her family. What a great heart the woman had to keep extending her hand and home to restless young girls, needing her guidance. Drape left her napkin in her chair and walked over to Mrs. Mack. "You've been the mother I never had."

Mrs. Mack stood and embraced Drape. "Never mind, never mind now. No one has a better profession than I do."

Ike tipped her head as if evaluating Mrs. Mack's role in her life. "No one could do it better, Mrs. Mack. You are always here for us without bludgeoning us to death with interference."

"Ike likes her independence," Stone said. "If you hadn't taken me under your wing, I don't know what would have happened to me."

Drape agreed with both of them and understood. Mrs. Mack was a further reason for Ike and Stone to stay close—in Ann Arbor. Blacky and Nosey took turns hugging Mrs. Mack, but Blacky looked at the world as though there were hundreds of Mrs. Macks just waiting to indulge her every whim. Nosey's self-confidence required no assistance from anyone so lowly as a sorority mother.

Drape did worry about Blacky and Nosey, even with Matt along for the Chicago move. They expected the world to meld to their wishes without fear of any consequences, rebuffs or hurdles. Drape hoped they were right and life would treat them well.

* * *

Saturday, January 19
Brighton Condo

Sky opened the condo door for Drape and her cronies.

Only Ike smiled at him. "What is this?" he asked. "Is someone ill?"

Drape frowned at him and then helped Stone off with her coat. "Stone hasn't heard from her mother for nine days. Mrs. Mack sent a detective to Evanston, but the police there don't know where she is, either."

Matt, who was as short as Blacky, gathered the girls' coats as they heaped them over his arms. "I worry about this old guy, Salvatore Bianco."

Nosey threw her coat over his head, but Blacky removed it, kissing the side of Matt's face and tenderly rumpling his shock of black hair. "You worry about every man within fifty miles of us."

23

"How old is Bianco?" Sky asked Drape.

"Over thirty, right, Stone?" Drape laughed.

Sky loved her laugh. He couldn't really find any fault with her. Bright and affectionate, she would be the perfect wife and mother—in just six months' time! His heart seemed to leap out of his chest whenever she was within sight. And she always knew how affected he was, smiling that secret, satisfied smile of hers. Was she teasing him now about this old guy? He kept eye contact, waiting for Stone to reply.

"Forty. I told you guys he's forty," Stone answered. "I'm sure Mother is fine. I've been keeping her in my prayers."

"That should do the trick," Sky said without thinking how Drape would respond.

She stared at him then patted Stone's shoulder. "I've been praying for His will to be done too."

"Do I detect a difference of prayer style?" Ike was always the kidder and nonbeliever,.

"Sorry," Sky said. "I find it difficult to share your thought processes when you talk about your belief system."

"I don't believe either," Nosey said. "I do support St. Andrew's to keep up its historic buildings."

Blacky nudged Sky's shoulder. "Nosey is duplicitous, Sky. I'm careful not to blaspheme before believers."

Stone seemed to wake from a daze. "Drape, have you told Sky about his appointment with Pastor Neiman?"

"Appointment?" Sky asked, realizing he'd stepped into moral quicksand.

"Not until three weeks before the wedding," Drape said.

Sky encircled Drape with his arms to capture her complete attention. "We understand each other, don't we?"

"We do," Drape said, stepping too close for all practical purposes with the crowd surrounding them.

Using the excuse of opening more salsa, Sky escaped into the kitchen.

The doorbell rang.

With a bowl of salsa in one hand Sky opened the door.

Mrs. Mack and a white-haired stranger stood on the condo's stoop. "Drape," Sky called for assistance, handing Drape the salsa.

Mrs. Mack explained as she stepped in. "Sky, this is Salvatore Bianco. He stopped by the sorority right after the girls left and I hoped you wouldn't mind if I brought him by to meet them."

Salvatore shed his leather coat, nodded to Sky and leaned toward Drape, righting the tipping bowl in her hand. "Who's this beauty?"

"My fiancé," Sky answered too loudly.

"Curtain Taylor," Drape said. "My friends call me Drape."

Salvatore handed the bowl back to Sky then turned to Drape, who was still standing too close in Sky's opinion. Then Salvatore even touched her hair! "Drape is a mysterious name for such a lovely woman."

Drape took his offered arm as Salvatore led her into the family room, sitting next to her on the couch.

Salvatore asked, "Now who among you lovely ladies is going to move into my apartment building?"

Nosey and Blacky raised their arms like obedient grammar-school girls.

Sky admitted the man was good looking. His white hair set off his blue eyes and olive skin. Salvatore bent his leg at the knee, like a woman, and swung his boot which was tipped with etched silver.

* * *

Drape's world stopped as soon as she saw Salvatore Bianco. At first she thought her awe was due to *not* having an older male in the house when she was younger, but she had never reacted to older professors the way she did toward this man.

Sky smelled clean like Irish Spring soap, but Salvatore's odor was of saffron. No, cedar. No, some incense … as if he'd attended a Roman Catholic high mass and hadn't changed his shirt. That wasn't exactly the smell, but she recognized it from some hallowed halls. So this was where the saying came from; her "nose was open" around this stranger. She just wasn't able to place the aroma. Too much else was happening around her and inside her nerve endings.

She couldn't ask Salvatore the make of his aftershave or soap, because Sky was hovering like a jealous bull.

Salvatore sat too close to her on the couch. When he swung his leg, his boot caught the hem of her skirt, moving it against her thigh awakening responses she'd never experienced before. Not with Sky.

25

Maybe she'd known Sky too long to feel this frisson of excitement. Was her entire body reacting to Salvatore's deliberate stimulus?

Drape scanned the room for Sky. On guard nearby, Sky extended his hand, rescuing her from the couch.

"Kitchen," Drape said, hoping to escape the intoxicating pull of this strange he-man, his smell, and her reactions to him, which would spoil her future, where there would be no wedding, no children, and no family if she let her body rule her now. She chose sanity, conjuring up Proverbs 2:7: "He layeth up sound wisdom for the righteous; he is a buckler for them that walk uprightly."

* * *

Sky backed Drape up to the opened refrigerator door. "What do you think of this guardian for the girls?"

"He's man enough," Drape gulped.

Sky shook her, and then apologized. "I don't know what's come over me." Then he kissed her as if he'd escaped from a desert and she was a well-spring. "I think he's evil incarnate," he said. "Isn't that a description of the devil?"

"You don't believe in heaven or hell," Drape said.

Matt joined them. "He'll be able to keep them safe." Matt rumpled his hair from worry. "If he doesn't harm them himself."

Sky couldn't let go of Drape. He stared at the butter tray over her head, waiting for her to reassure him.

"You're etched in my heart," Drape finally said.

"Etched?" he asked, thinking: *like in stone*. Was her heart now moving with stony resolve to wed him?

"I need to drive you home, please," Sky pleaded.

"Of course," Drape said, "but we need to join our guests."

Stone was standing near the entrance. "I'd like to go home, Drape. I'm not feeling well."

Sky wasn't feeling too good himself.

Drape called to Mrs. Mack. "Will you drive my Mustang back with Stone?"

Mrs. Mack bent down to look at Stone. Normally, she hugged her charges but Stone couldn't abide being touched. "Find your coat, dear. We'll leave as soon as I give my keys to Salvatore to drive the girls home."

Matt objected. "I'll drive Blacky."

"Ike," Mrs. Mack called, "will you and Nosey show Salvatore how to get to the train station. His suitcase is still in the trunk of my car."

* * *

Drape felt confused by the rush to get back to Ann Arbor. "Why didn't we ask Salvatore about Stone's mother?"

"Why didn't Stone?"

"The other girls were taking all of Salvatore's time with questions about the apartment, I guess." Drape remembered Stone's white face. "Was she jealous? He didn't even talk to her, did he?" Drape remembered Salvatore's low tones the focus of his delving eyes.

"I was too interested in your responses to notice."

"See," Drape explained. "This is exactly where my religion saved the day."

"How is that?" Sky challenged.

"Well," Drape waved her arm to dispense any of the smell still lingering in her memory of Salvatore's scent. "You know he's attractive. Are we having our first fight?" Drape ignored the truths tugging at her soul.

"I'm asking for reassurance, again."

"Never fear. I've chosen you, and we have a date for our future."

"Is that the date when we let our passion for each other finally blossom?" Sky's voice was too soft.

"Our love took root a long time ago. And we're going to see a garden of such magnificence, even I can't guarantee you won't call for a gardener to cut back on the exuberant blooms."

"Good enough," Sky said. "That's good enough for me."

"Why did Salvatore bring a suitcase?" Drape asked, knowing it was a question with no answer, at least not in the foreseeable future.

Chapter Three

Thursday, February 14
Sigma Kappa House

Sky knocked on the sorority-house door, clutching a heart-shaped box of chocolates with a dozen red roses in the crook of his arm. He'd agreed with Drape about her thesis being a priority, which meant she put off visiting him or even telling her mother and grandmother the dates for her shower and the wedding. Drape had divulged her engagement on Christmas Eve, but promised her family to delay marriage until her education was completed.

Two days earlier, Drape had presented her final thesis to Professor Hazzard and then called and visited Sky to celebrate. They had spoken daily, but Sky hadn't seen her since the party in January when Salvatore Bianco had showed up unexpectedly.

The night before, Sky convinced Drape to call her family in Florida about her thesis completion and the upcoming marriage schedule. Her grandmother promised to come visit immediately so she could finally meet him in person and help Drape prepare for the wedding.

Today, unfortunately, Salvatore Bianco opened the Sigma Kappa Sorority's front door. "Sky, right? Come in, come in."

"Drape?" That was all Sky could muster.

Salvatore slapped his back. "In the dining room. Mother Taylor and Grandma are giving her a thorough examination."

Drape entered the foyer, taking the flowers and chocolates out of Sky's hands. "Salvatore stayed in town to get to know Nosey and Blacky better."

Salvatore Bianco had waltzed back into the dining room, where various female voices excitedly called his name.

"Last night," Sky said. "You didn't mention Salvatore was still in town. How long has he been here?"

"Since your party," Drape said. "Come meet Grandma and Mother. This morning Mrs. Mack had served them breakfast before I even knew they'd arrived."

Sky pulled her into his arms. His mind was a blank. It was Valentine's Day. Drape struggled against him, not like the night before when her kisses had been sweet and inviting. With her doctorate thesis under her belt, she'd seemed triumphant. Last night she'd talked about her next goal to start a family with *him* in five months' time.

"My folks," Drape said, fluffing her soft hair.

He hadn't touched her hair. Her perfume was different from the night before. She was already walking away from him.

Stone Slager approached slowly, taking the flowers out of Drape's hands in a solemn manner as if they were meant for display on a coffin.

"Your mother?" Sky asked.

Stone shrugged her shoulders. "No word from Detective Combs. He's still in Chicago. I'll put these in water."

"Look what Sky has brought us," Drape said as she entered the dining room.

"They're for you," Sky said. What, was he crazy? Of course she'd share. Everything was wrong. He turned to go. He didn't want to meet her parents, not with Salvatore Bianco in the same room.

His hand was on the front door knob, but Ike stepped between him and the door. "You don't want to leave, do you?"

He stared at Ike. "Her parents met Salvatore."

"Grandma's not happy," Ike said.

Sky had only spoken to the woman on the phone, but he already cherished the grandmother's loyalty. "Good. What about you?"

Ike pointed him toward the dining room, speaking softly, "Oh, Salvatore's democratic with his attention. Spreads it around, thick and meaningless."

Sky smiled, astonished his face remembered how.

Ike announced his entrance like a referee at a boxing match:, "And in this corner, the heart-rending contender, Cosmos Henderson! We call him Sky because his ideals are high and his heart true."

Drape laughed louder than the rest. She was on the other side of the table unwrapping *his* chocolates with Salvatore's help.

Grandma Taylor, the same size as Drape, presented herself. She first took Sky's hand, and then she reached up to bend his neck so she could plant a kiss on his cheek. She whispered, "You're a good looking man, Sky. I can see why Drape chose you."

Mother Taylor wore a short black wool dress. She nodded from her seat against the wall near the buffet, where she was energetically swinging her crossed leg. Her black, high-heeled boot reminded Sky of Salvatore's silver-tipped boots.

Sky walked over to his intended's mother and offered his hand.

Ignoring his extended hand, Mother Taylor said, "Sit down at the table, Sky. You look like you could use a cup of coffee, if not a pot. Do you recognize, 'Now see that noble and most sovereign reason, like sweet bells jangled, out of tune and harsh?'"

Sky thought Shakespeare might have entered the fray, but he couldn't place the quote. He took her advice and chose a chair across the table from Drape.

Mrs. Mack bustled about, pouring Sky orange juice, asking if he wanted sausage or bacon to go with the plate of scrambled eggs she was preparing him from the buffet's offerings.

"Bacon," Sky said, noticing Nosey had moved between Salvatore and Drape and taken her time choosing which truffle she wanted.

Drape met his eyes. "Salvatore moved in next door at the Sigma Chi fraternity." Then she explained to Mother Taylor: "Sky didn't join a fraternity."

No money. Sky wanted to shout, but stuffed his mouth with a hot English muffin. He smiled at Mother Taylor, who continued to stare at him.

Grandma asked Blacky to switch chairs with her and started a monologue, which Sky tuned-in to intermittently. "The girls—sorry, the young sorority sisters—have taken care of nearly every detail of the shower and wedding."

Sky wondered if they'd changed the groom without notifying him.

"Where are you going on your honeymoon?" Grandma asked.

The room went quiet. Even Salvatore stopped talking to Nosey, dropping his hand from Drape's shoulder to listen to Sky's answer.

"We want to start a family," Sky said, convinced he'd suddenly descended into retardation.

Drape explained, "He means we're going to honeymoon in our condo in Brighton."

"No," Mother Taylor said, "you're both going to tour Europe. Drape, you know we've talked about this before. Shakespeare recommends the tour somewhere, I'm sure."

Drape shook her head at Sky, but he suddenly thought it was a great idea. "Is Salvatore coming too?" he asked, completely insane with jealousy.

Blacky took Salvatore's hand, and Nosey followed the pair out of the dining room. Mrs. Mack looked down at her napkin ready to dry her eyes with it. Mother Taylor continued to stare.

Drape made an attempt to explain Sky's rudeness. "I didn't tell Sky that Salvatore hadn't returned to Chicago. He's just shocked to see him here."

Stone entered the deadly quiet dining room, carrying the red roses. She stood at the doorway and then dropped the vase. "Has Combs called?"

Mrs. Mack flew into action, sweeping up the fallen bouquet, grabbing napkins for the pool of water, and setting the unbroken vase on the table. "No, Stone, sorry. Detective Combs hasn't called this morning. Sky is upset to see Salvatore still here."

* * *

Drape nodded to her mother and then walked around the long table to sit next to Sky. "I didn't know my folks or Salvatore would be here this morning." It didn't help. Poor Sky was mortified by his behavior. "Let's take Mother and Grandma to Brighton, show them our condo."

Sky stood, walking like a zombie toward the front door. "Good idea."

At Sky's van, Grandma pushed Drape away from the front passenger door. "Sit in the back with your mother. I want to get to know this young man."

Obediently, Drape fastened her seat belt in the back seat. Already she'd completely ruined Valentine's Day for Sky. The truth was she *had* hidden Salvatore Bianco's continued presence in Ann Arbor from Sky when they spoke on the telephone each night. She'd told herself she didn't want to worry Sky. But maybe she didn't want to explain that she'd enjoyed seeing Salvatore almost every day at the sorority. Blacky and Nosey vied for the older man's attention. However, Drape had noticed Salvatore would stop conversations with either of them whenever she returned from the museum.

Salvatore was good for her ego. In her thoughts she often substituted "Daddy" for Salvatore and hoped she would *not* make any such slip in her speech. When she'd introduced him to her zoology and paleontology professors, they were clearly impressed with his knowledge of how they prepared and catalogued the wide range of specimen bones.

Professor Leland gave Salvatore a thorough tour of the research museum not open to the public, including the two sub-basements. "We were originally called the Cabinet of Curiosities." Leland smiled proudly at Drape. "Now we are among the largest mammal collections in the world."

Even Professor Jane Hazzard commented on Salvatore's Italian good looks. "He knows how to own a suit of clothes."

And Salvatore completely understood why Drape *didn't* want to leave the Zoology Museum after she graduated. Sky knew she'd applied for a lecturing position, but Salvatore really empathized with her attachment to the building itself.

Salvatore had touched the wood storage cabinets in the halls, remarking on their beauty. "The Field Museum's back rooms are not as impressive."

For Drape, the museum was more of a home than the sorority. She'd spent significantly more hours awake in these spacious marble halls. Grandma had been correct. Sixteen was too early to start a life on her own. When Mother and Grandma sold their home in Seattle to move to Florida, Drape's brain dove into her studies to avoid the feelings of loss. The least they could have done was stay together, but they ended up in Vero Beach and Fort Lauderdale, because they couldn't agree on the benefits each city afforded.

This morning's scripture was Proverbs 2:11, and it teased her: "Discretion shall preserve thee, understanding shall keep thee."

In the front of the van, Grandma settled back in her seat apparently giving up trying to carry on a conversation with just monosyllables from Sky. She turned slightly to address Drape. "Tell me about your sorority sisters, Drape. Nosey and Blacky seem quite taken with Salvatore. I thought you told me Blacky and Matt North were engaged."

"Not quite," Sky interjected.

"Salvatore's trying to reassure Nosey and Blacky that Chicago will be a safe place to work," Drape said.

"Why do all the girls have gender-neutral names?" Mother asked.

Drape held her temper. Curtain was certainly a gender-neutral name. It was no name at all! "Ike's real name is Katrina, but she didn't want to be nicknamed Kat or Trina, so she made up Ike. Blacky hated her name Holly, because people made so many Christmas jokes. Stone's mother is a bit odd. I guess because Stone was so unresponsive as a baby, she nicknamed her Stone. Her real name is Shelby. Nosey is a family name."

Calmed down by the recitation, Drape attempted to lift Sky's mood too. "Sky, remember Ike always says Nosey was hatched?" No response. She plodded on, "We found out she was born at home on a farm in Indiana. Her birth certificate says the farm was in Dry Grove Township and her parents took two years to register her birth."

"All you girls are so intelligent," Grandma said. "Do Blacky and Nosey have PhDs?"

"I'm the only odd ball," Drape said. "Mrs. Mack let me stay after graduation because of my age."

"I should hope so," Mother said.

Drape looked at her. Did Mother realize how unusual it was to be twenty years old with a doctorate degree only months away? "How old were you when you graduated?"

Mother patted her knee. "I only have a Masters in English, Curtain. I was twenty-two by the time I finished my thesis."

"Shakespeare addict," Grandma said, poking Sky, who did not react. "What do Nosey and Blacky's parents think of their moving to Chicago?"

"Have no idea," Drape said. "They're probably happy they found jobs with only a Bachelor's degree under their belts."

Mother asked, "How old are they?"

"I'm the youngest. Stone is twenty-one, Ike soon will be." Drape wondered if she would be more emotionally mature in two or three years. "Nosey and Blacky are both twenty-two."

Sky spoke up. "I'm twenty-four, if anyone is interested."

At least he wasn't having any trouble managing the van on the winter roads, which were dry after the previous day's snowstorm. Drape wanted Sky to keep talking, but he was still too angry.

From the heavy silence, Grandma must have surmised the same fact. "Tell me a little more about Matt North, Drape."

"Native-American. Mrs. Mack calls him Mr.-Fix-It. He helps around the sorority, plumbing, broken windows, you know. Blacky took pity on him. He was mad for Ike, but she dumped him when she gained an inch on his height."

"Rather shallow." Grandma made a tsk noise.

"But her sense of humor is delightful," Mother said.

"She and Stone are trying to find jobs in Ann Arbor at the university. They love the town as much as I do."

Sky turned and sent a confused look in her direction. "I thought you liked our condo."

"It's perfect." Drape hastened to add, "Grandma, you'll see what I mean, and the condo is half-way between Lansing and Ann Arbor. We'll both have the same amount of commute time."

"Do you enjoy teaching, Sky?" Mother asked.

Sky nodded. "Two of my statistical papers are being published in March."

"Good work," Grandma said.

* * *

Brighton Condo

Sky rattled the pots and pans louder than was necessary to drown out the female voices from the family room. They were driving him crazy. Maybe he was meant to live alone. He'd have the time and the quiet to become a world-class mathematician.

His temper was still blowing his thoughts to worthless whiffs of sense. For instance, he hadn't told Drape his parents were coming for dinner. Maybe he should just surprise her! He looked into the living room but Mother Taylor pointed upstairs.

* * *

God bless Grandmas everywhere, Drape prayed. Hers noticed the racket in the kitchen without rolling her eyes like Mother.

"Show me the upstairs," Grandma had said, pinching Drape's shoulder to get her attention.

Upstairs, Grandma sat down on the double bed prepared to listen for eternity.

Drape felt more like crying than talking. "I love him."

"I know. Men can seem a little strange at times." Grandma waved vaguely at the bedroom door. "Especially when they don't expect an older, good-looking suitor to be living so close to their fiancée."

"Salvatore's not courting me." Drape wasn't as sure as she sounded. Why did Salvatore dog her every step in Ann Arbor, call her each evening to see if she'd gone to Lansing or stayed at the sorority to work on her thesis? He was interested in Blacky or Nosey, wasn't he? But he had talked to the Museum Director, Professor Carl Foster, about the need for security measures as though he were applying for a job as a night guard. She didn't remember how long he'd attended the university as a young man, but Salvatore did say Ann Arbor was his kind of town. "Besides, he's not the courting type."

"You're right there." Grandma hadn't moved from the bed.

Gaining confidence as she spoke, Drape said. "He's old. You know what they say about older men."

"I don't."

"Their sperm is aged and children could be retarded or deformed." Drape noticed Grandma's eyes got a lot bigger than was necessary.

Sky spoke behind her. "You're as bad as your mother. Worse! I'm a human being not a sperm bank."

He came in, muscling his way past Grandma's knees, took Drape's hand and pulled his engagement ring from her finger. He stood there for a minute, turned his back and said, "Now come down and meet your new in-laws."

Grandma was on her feet almost running to catch Sky, but he was too quick for her.

"Now what do I do?"

"Meet your new in-laws." Grandma hugged her, and then slapped her behind. "You and I are staying in this house until that ring is back on your finger."

* * *

Downstairs, Sky just hoped his mother would not comment on the color of his ears, which were burning. "Mother Taylor, please meet my parents, Geraldine and James Henderson."

"How do you do," Geraldine said. "I haven't met your daughter, Drape."

"Curtain," Mother Taylor said. "Drape is her sorority sisters' nickname for her."

"And mine." Sky smiled at Drape as she came down the stairs with her Grandma behind her, almost shoving her forward. She was adorable. How had they quarreled? It didn't matter. He loved her. Surely she knew he loved her down to her socks even if he'd been so mean the minute before.

Sky's father embraced Drape. "Oh, don't be shy with me. I hug everybody, don't I, Geraldine?"

"He does, he does," Geraldine gushed. "Drape, you are lovely. And I hear your brains outshine your beauty."

"Never a better compliment. I'm Mrs. Richard Taylor, Drape's grandmother. My husband was into railroad bonds. The good kind."

Sky wrinkled his brow at the comment about Grandma's source of money.

"Oh, I don't mind, Sky," Grandma said. "I wouldn't want your parents to allow you to marry Drape without knowing where her family came from."

Mother Taylor coughed.

"I've explained about Drape's birth," Sky said, taking Drape's cold hand, slipping the engagement ring into the palm of her hand.

"And did they approve of my ingenious solution?" Mother Taylor asked, patting the seat on the couch next to her when Sky's father extended his hand. "Cleopatra said it best, 'Riotous madness, to be entangled with those mouth-made vows.'"

"Good men are hard to find," Geraldine said.

Grandma took Geraldine's arm, and they sat next to Mother Taylor after shooing Sky's father off the couch. "And your Sky is one of them."

"He's the best," Drape said, a little too loudly for the occasion. "Do I smell toast?"

"No," Sky panicked. "Burnt roast."

* * *

After a dinner of well-done beef, scalloped potatoes, peas, and chocolate cake, Drape wasn't surprised when Grandma demonstrated she had more tricks up her sleeve.

Grandma started quietly enough. "My granddaughter, daughter and I are all Episcopalians. I looked up St. Andrew's Civil War history, Drape. You couldn't have chosen a more regal church for the wedding. Have you met with Pastor Nieman yet?"

Geraldine was in the kitchen with Sky, but she came back to stand next to her husband. "We didn't raise our son to adopt a religious crutch."

Drape wanted to run, but Mother placed her hand on Drape's lap. "My mother taught me to cultivate an attitude of gratitude, which I passed on to Drape."

James Henderson nodded. "The hypocrites who attend churches are not good examples of integrity for Cosmos or Drape."

Without raising her eyes to address anyone in particular, Drape said, "I made a list of five things I was grateful for every day since I was seven. While we still lived in Seattle, I realized I was thankful *to* someone or something. I started attending St. Andrew's in Ann Arbor because I wanted others to know how good the Lord has been to me. Matt North, Blacky's friend, met me while he was dating Ike. I was grieving the loss of my home in Washington—my folks had moved to Florida. Angry and fearful, I could hardly study. Matt knew I was upset." Drape looked around the table. "He sat down with me one day, after Ike dumped him. He reminded me the Lord doesn't want us to be unhappy. He died so we could live the life we were put on earth to live.

"Then Matt asked me to accept the Lord's gift—that he died so we could live freely. With his instruction as to the meaning of John 3:16, I invited the Savior into my life. I will never forget the immediate sense of calm. Writers have called it the oceanic feeling of oneness with the universe. All I knew was that all was right with the world and God was in his heaven. Now I strive and pray each day to trust the Lord more."

Sky left the dishes to their own devices and joined her at the table. "Drape doesn't worry about my soul. Do you?"

Drape raised her head to speak to his parents. "The Bible says anyone who gives a cup of water to a believer is saved too. Besides, the souls of other people are not my business. I don't know how to reach or teach them. I can talk about how I came to receive the gift of faith, but nothing more."

Geraldine had drawn out the chair at the head of the table. "Will Pastor Nieman want assurances you will raise the children as believers?"

Grandma laughed. "You're thinking about old Roman Catholic rules. Episcopalians are free thinkers. When we say the creed at mass, we use the plural pronoun because someone in the congregation may actually believe each and every edict. We encourage doubts to vocalize what believing is. It is a gift. No one can reach for faith with reason up their sleeves."

Sky made his comments directly to his parents too. "Drape tells me I'm etched in her heart. Apparently, that is the only thing written in stone in this house. Our children will be free to find their own direction."

Grandma regained their attention. "Sky is the soul of integrity and has a heart filled with love for Drape. Could any of us ask for more?"

A few hours later Sky's parents said their goodbyes, after admiring Drape's newly redecorated ring finger. Sky put on his coat to take Drape and her folks back to Ann Arbor.

"Drape and I are staying with you until the wedding, Sky." Grandma handed their coats back to him. "My daughter will find an expensive hotel to stay at here in Brighton. Take her with you to pack up Drape's clothing."

Sky seemed to understand Grandma's motives sooner than Drape did. Whose brain was supposed to be quicker, hers or Sky's? He embraced Grandma and then Drape. "We'll be right back. I have a sleeping bag I can use on the couch."

"Fine," Grandma said. "Isn't that fine?"

Mother nodded, accustomed to Grandma getting her way without argument. "Curtain, you can tell the girls goodbye later."

Drape wondered when that would be. Would she be allowed? Allowed? When had that word last been heard in her brain? "What about the trip to Chicago to see where the girls are going to live? We have tickets for the Goodman play, *Measure for Measure*."

"March twenty-second, right?" Sky asked, smiling for all he was worth.

He was handsome, after all. And Drape didn't love him *just* because he would make great looking babies, but he would. Her arms ached for them, the promised babies, even as she waved goodbye to their prospective father.

CHAPTER FOUR

Brighton Condo

Sky was exhausted after packing and hauling all of Drape's belongings to Brighton. Mother Taylor hadn't been much help. She had pointed to the clothing to be boxed and opened Drape's dresser drawers at the sorority house, but other than that she did very little bundling and no hauling at all.

Mother Taylor avoided the work by talking nonstop about Drape's childhood, all sixteen years of it. It was as if she had hung onto every breath and word out of the poor girl's mouth. No wonder his fiancée had felt abandoned when Mother Taylor and Drape's grandmother left the Seattle area and moved to Florida. Now the two women even lived in separate towns down there. Sky could provide Drape with all the creature comforts in their home, but he understood too how important Mother Taylor and Grandma were to Drape, and how devoted to her they were. His own parents were more hands off about his wellbeing. Maybe having two parents spread the responsibility around enough to relax them around their offspring.

Mother Taylor had said the Campus Inn in Ann Arbor was good enough for her, so Sky drove back to Brighton by himself. When he arrived, Grandma and Drape were busy chatting and rearranging the dishes in the kitchen cupboards, so he lugged in all the boxes of Drape's belongings.

Relegated to the sofa, Sky slept on his right side. His left, deaf ear shut out the continuing conversation upstairs between his fiancée and her grandmother. As soon as his head hit the couch pillow, visions of his future filled his dreams.

The dreams came fast and furious. A naming committee of three women sat on a stage behind a lace-draped table demanding answers from Drape and him. They were seated in the lower orchestra pit.

Drape suggested two Christian names, "Ann and Sue for the girls."

Mother Taylor approved. "Single syllable names discourage nicknames."

"Could be boys," Grandma said.

"Bob and Sam?" Sky humbly suggested, not willing to be shot down by his mother or the women in Drape's family -- even in a dreamscape.

Geraldine, his mother, shook her head. "Bob is too common. How about Jake and Ted?"

"I don't like Sue," Sky ventured.

Drape hit his shoulder. "This is hard enough without you turning against me."

Sky felt his courage return. After all, they were only in a dream. "You probably want to call our son, Sal, after Salvatore Bianco."

Grandma waved her hand. "I like Ruth better than Sue."

Drape smiled that satisfied grin she knew overwhelmed all his physical faculties, including his brain. "Ann and Ruth and Ted and Sam."

The dream committee and thousands in the audience clapped in agreement. Sky rolled over on the narrow couch, hugging his pillow as he hoped to hug Drape in a few more months.

* * *

Friday, February 15

After Sky left for work, Drape attacked the mess he had dumped in the living room. Her belongings were strewn all over the place. Clothes on hangers draped over the dining room chairs. Suitcases and an assortment of odd cardboard boxes—boxes Mrs. Mack had probably saved for just such moving emergencies—littered nearly every available floor space. Some were even stacked three high against the walls in the hall.

"Grandma," Drape called. "Where shall I start?"

Grandma pulled out a dining room chair. "Phone," she said. "And pour me another cup of coffee."

Within the hour, a crew of four painters had moved all of Drape's belongings to the basement, covered the existing furniture downstairs and upstairs and started painting the walls. Drape wanted to wait for

Sky's opinions, but Grandma insisted they didn't have time for a color-blind male to pick out shades of paint.

Then Drape was dragged along to three furniture stores, where Grandma allowed one phone call to Sky, who said anything they chose was fine with him. He'd been walking into his classroom when they called. He did ask for matching recliners. So off they went, buying a new dining room table with padded chairs and a matching china cabinet, two bedrooms suites, a new couch, complementary colored recliners, lamps, pillows and even an entryway coat tree and boot bench. Immediate delivery and removal of the existing furniture were Grandma's only condition to the sales.

By two o'clock the painters had finished, the furniture was all in place and Grandma had paid the movers to haul Drape's belongings to the upstairs bedrooms.

After they left, Grandma excused herself for a nap on the new couch.

Drape attacked the job of putting away her possessions. She stored her spring and summer wardrobes in the walk-in closet of the master bedroom. She couldn't help thinking about Sky warming up the master bed until their honeymoon. Her fall and winter clothes she hung in the guest bedroom she was sharing with Grandma.

As Drape unrolled her poetry posters on the twin beds, Grandma surprised her. "Better decorate the basement with them. You and Sky should select paintings you both enjoy for the walls."

"Blacky's posters are always of pink flamingos. Isn't that funny?"

"She probably misses Florida more than she admits. Your poetry posters always show leafed out trees, streams and birds. One would think you didn't enjoy winter's beauty."

"Nosey's prints are consistently of tanned and oiled men in various stages of undress."

"She does focus on the physical. What about Ike and Stone?"

"None of us were ever allowed in Stone's room, but Ike's are of the glories of winter you were extolling."

"I am curious about Stone's posters," Grandma said. "Poor thing. She misses her mother even though they don't seem to have been that close."

"I think Mrs. Mack has mothered her more than anyone in her life."

Grandma held her hand as Drape reached for another armload of sweaters. "And you have patterned a lot of your new behavior after Mrs. Mack's."

"I have not, have I?"

"You brush off your jeans the same way Mrs. Mack dusts her skirts when she doesn't want to take responsibility for something."

"Really? I should have color coordinated everything. I've touched every article of clothing and accessory I own." Drape hugged her grandmother, breathing in the comforting smell of her old-fashioned Arpege perfume. "The master bedroom dressers you bought us all have a shallow top drawer for jewelry, and so do the bedside tables."

"We probably should have moved the vanity into the guest bedroom," Grandma said. "Until you're married."

"I don't mind Sky seeing me without makeup if we're going to live together until we get old."

"It's till death, honey."

"I know, Grandma. I mean, Sky might as well see the real me."

* * *

Friday, March 8
Henderson's Home in Lansing

To Drape, the austere grey brick façade with graveled trim beneath low hedges negated any hope of a warm welcome at her future in-laws' house.

But Geraldine Henderson's dining room outshone Mrs. Mack's. Half-moon stained-glass windows with various intricate rose patterns topped each of the tall, windowed walls of the circular room. The chandelier seemed to mirror the windows' fluctuating colors if not those of the centerpiece, heaped with a plethora of different colored roses. The crystal glassware mimicked the chandelier's ability to reflect myriad hues. In jarring contrast to the glassware, the plates and bowls were thick and old-fashioned, unmatched and clashing on the red tablecloth. Even the napkins failed to match any color scheme. Drape's fingers itched to rearrange the settings so that they would at least not clash with the neighboring dishes.

Seating for twelve around the traditional rectangular table promised lively conversation for the meal. Across the table from Sky, Mother was seated on Geraldine's right, while Grandma had the seat of honor next to the host's right, facing Drape. Next to Drape, Mrs. Mack, Ike and Stone sat across the table from Blacky, Matt and Nosey.

Jim Henderson spoke first. "So we will not say grace over this stuffed Cornish hen dinner, even though some of our guests are encouraged to silently bless our meal."

Nosey asked, "Are we allowed to speak about politics and sex if the calmer subject of religion is barred?"

"Religion has never been a soothing topic," Geraldine said. "And opposing belief systems caused most of the wars throughout the centuries."

"Sex has started a few wars too," Mother added. "And motivated our Anglican Church to break away from the Romans."

"Oh, but not our peaceful politicians," Drape said. "They would never let themselves be seduced by the military-industrial complex that paid their way into office."

"Refuge in politeness is never the mark of a coward," Mrs. Mack said.

"And the nice thing about truth," Grandma said quietly, "it will always will its way out."

Stone's voice could barely be heard by the rest of the room. "Mother's been missing for too long. I know what that means. When do you all think my mother's murderer will be found?"

"Soon," Matt said before the others could recover. "Mrs. Slager's killer will find justice swift and sure, if she's come to harm."

"Neither," Ike said. "Justice is for the rich to wreak upon the poor."

"I hope not," Drape said, "or what is life worth?"

Sky assumed the champion's role. "Life is for living and for establishing families to guard and protect each other."

"To life," Blacky said, raising her glass.

And they all toasted the day, "To life!"

* * *

Friday, March 15
Brighton Condo

At the breakfast counter, Drape and Sky enjoyed a second cup of coffee before Grandma joined them the day of Drape's scheduled doctoral defense.

"The blue walls in the family room are rather elegant," Drape said.

"Better than the gray that white walls always turn into after Michigan winters." Sky arranged his briefcase for class where it sat on the stool next to him. "Red's a bit bright for the kitchen."

"Grandma says it should act as a stop sign for both of us. She doesn't think we should spend time cooking when we could be exercising or reading something challenging."

"By the way." Sky reached behind her neck, pulling her toward him for a kiss. "You look very professional this morning. And, I do love the reclining sectional." Then he whispered, "After we're home from the honeymoon, evenings could be quite interesting making babies in the family room. We should eat together at the dining room table as often as possible. Families need to face each other every day to stay connected and happy."

Drape kissed Sky again. Her future husband did know how a real family should live. "You don't mind sleeping in the big bed by yourself?"

"Temporarily." Sky chuckled. "I wish I could come to your thesis defense, but assistant professors aren't wise to arrange substitutes for their first class assignment. Are you and Grandma comfortable in the guest room beds? Nice of her to furnish the place, especially to our taste."

"What's money for?" Grandma said, pushing Sky's closed briefcase off the stool onto the floor. "If you can't spend it on people you love? Drape, those thigh-high boots are very becoming."

Drape kissed Sky goodbye while inwardly blessing him with Proverbs 2:20: "That thou mayest walk in the way of good men, and keep the paths of righteousness."

* * *

Zoology Museum

In the paneled conference room, where a secretary had placed silk lilacs in the bricked-up fireplace grill, Drape's fifteen-minute defense of her thesis went extremely well. Professor Chinich asked two questions about her final graph, but Professor Clarke answered for her as she clicked the large screen to three additional slides she'd prepared in case the final graph needed further clarification.

Professor Clarke rose and escorted her to the door. She wondered if she had convinced the group that the data from over two hundred years showed changes in the fox species, specifically modifications in skull dimensions. After receiving a nod and a smile from Professor Hazzard, her advisor, Drape left the room to wait outside for the verdict.

Loitering in the hall were Ike, Blacky and Nosey. Ike was a head taller than Blacky. Nosey was even shorter than Grandma. Grandma had seen Drape leave the seminar room too. But Stone and Salvatore were facing away from her.

Salvatore was saying rather loudly to Stone, "Don't ever ask me about your mother!"

In spite of her distress, Stone must have noticed the other girls were staring at Drape standing behind her. "Oh, Drape," she said, turning. "Congratulations. Sorry about upsetting Salvatore."

"Salvatore?" Drape asked. "You're the one we should be thinking of. It's been three months!"

Salvatore nearly pushed Stone aside. "Congratulations, Drape."

"They haven't decided yet." Drape wanted to put her arms around Stone, but she knew Stone hated being touched. "Have you heard lately from Detective Combs?"

Stone nodded. "Her Evanston apartment neighbors haven't seen her. They said she was going to teach them origami, but wasn't home on Saturday the nineteenth. That's when Salvatore showed up with Mrs. Mack at Sky's party, remember?"

Grandma wasn't aware of Stone's aversion to touch. She brushed Stone's unruly hair away from her face before opening her arms for a hug. The girls drew in a synchronized breath, but Stone stepped into Grandma's arms, weeping silently. "Drape," Grandma patted Stone's back as if she needed a burp, "The girls will stay here with you. Salvatore, you can help me take Stone back to the sorority house, since you're the one to make her cry."

"Me?" Salvatore spread his arms, at a loss for words for probably the first time in his life.

"Stone," Drape said, "you and Grandma can find out how long Salvatore knew your mother. Is Detective Combs still at the sorority?"

"Mrs. Mack," Stone mumbled. "She's fixing lunch for us all, including Combs."

The professors filed out of the conference room. Professor Clarke walked up to Grandma, who still held Stone's hand. "Your granddaughter made us all proud."

Drape hugged Professor Hazzard and shook all the other committee members' hands. "I think I'm somewhat in shock."

Professor Foster congratulated her and added, "I expect you to take over Professor Pollack's calculus class permanently in the fall. His wife called this morning to say he's had another stroke."

"I'm so sorry," Drape said. Her future was secure. Now she could concentrate on her friends' dilemmas and on her own wedding. "You'll all be receiving invitations to my wedding in June. Thank you for all your time and graciousness."

"Tut, tut," Professor Leland said. "Salvatore, aren't you proud of your fiancée?"

Drape shook her head at Grandma. "No, Professor Leland. Salvatore's not my fiancé. You remember Cosmos Henderson? He's my fiancé."

Professor Clarke patted her shoulder. "We get everything mixed up at our age." He propelled Professor Leland down the hall.

"We'll see you girls at the sorority house," Grandma said, nearly pushing Salvatore out the exit door to the steps.

Nosey looked close to tears. "Your grandmother shouldn't treat Salvatore so harshly. He's upset about Stone's mother too. You know he's giving us an inordinate amount of time to feel confident in our new Chicago home. And, he's given both of us invaluable information about our jobs at the Field Museum. I'm amazed you're not aware of his status, even if he is only their night guard."

"Didn't look troubled in the least," Ike said. "How about you, Blacky? Is Matt's replacement distraught?"

"You are such a bear." Blacky had changed hairstyles from loose and curly to brushed sleek into a tight bun, but her lovely face still resembled a Botticelli angel. "Give it a break." Blacky took Drape's hand. "We need to celebrate with Drape. Is Sky coming?"

"Working." Drape pulled her scarf closer around her coat collar as they walked to the sorority house. Spring was supposed to be five days away, but the Northern Junko hadn't moved north. *Please, Lord*, she prayed. *Please help us find Stone's mother soon.*

* * *

Friday, March 22
Chicago Bound Train

The Goodman Theatre's scheduling of '*Measure for Measure*' coincided with Detective Combs' request for help from Stone's friends to search for her mother. Ike had lunch with them at the train-station's restaurant, the Gandy Dancer. But Mrs. Mack, Mother and Ike excused themselves from the investigative trip to finish addressing Drape's shower and wedding invitations.

On the train Grandma commandeered the aisle seat next to Drape, after asking Salvatore to get up and move to the seat across the aisle. Nosey was only too happy to curl up next to him. Combs sat opposite Nosey with Stone directly facing Salvatore. Blacky and Matt faced Grandma and Drape.

"Why did everyone clap when the train went by in the restaurant?" Grandma had wanted to know. "The Gandy Dancer's a bit upscale for such rowdy behavior."

"Tradition," Matt said. "You can't carry on much of a conversation as the trains thunder by, so we celebrate."

Salvatore laughed. "I like everything about Ann Arbor. Even the weather is milder."

"Then why didn't you stay here?" Nosey asked. "After you graduated?"

Salvatore ignored her and recrossed his legs when Detective Combs repeated the question, "Why did you leave?"

"The Field Museum's reputation seduced me," Salvatore said.

"Seduction has always been an easy answer." Grandma hit Salvatore's shoulder.

Drape coughed at her grandmother's double message. "Who's read the play, '*Measure for Measure*'? Now there's some serious seduction."

"Virtue on trial." Grandma nodded.

"Isn't it the play that inspired the opera *Tosca*?" Nosey asked Salvatore.

"I don't attend opera," Salvatore said.

"Different ending." Drape wondered why even the play might not be a safe topic of conversation. Grandma and Salvatore were at odds about almost everything. This morning's reading from Proverbs seemed foreboding too: "Let not mercy and truth forsake thee: bind them about your neck; write them down upon the tables of your heart." Would this trip to uncover the whereabouts of Stone's mother cause truth to flee the scene?

"How long did you know Mrs. Slager?" the detective asked.

"Who?" Salvatore pointed across the aisle to Drape's window. "Deer!"

They all craned to catch a glimpse, but apparently only Salvatore had been so honored.

"Stone's mother?" Detective Combs repeated.

"We dated while she lived in my apartment building. Nice woman. I think her new boyfriend talked her into moving to Evanston."

Combs took out his laptop. "Do you remember his name?"

"George. I know the last name. Can't recall it right now. Stone, do you remember his name?"

"I don't remember a George." Stone tugged at her matted hair as if she was trying to pull out the answer. "Mother wasn't dating anyone when I visited her new apartment for Christmas. She was playing MahJongg with three of her new neighbors. Maybe they would know George's last name."

"And how long did you date," Detective Combs was obviously good at his job, not letting go of his line of questioning.

Salvatore pointed at Stone. "Not a year, was it?"

Nosey answered for Stone, "Your mother lived at Salvatore's place in the summer, remember?"

Stone nodded. "That's when we met Salvatore."

Combs made a note. "About six months, would you say?"

"I think that's right," Salvatore smiled at everyone. "I hope you all like the restaurants I chose for dinner tonight. Have you attended progressive dinners? We'll eat seafood at 'The Dock.' They serve the fish on a piece of wood, a plank surrounded by mashed potato waves. Then we'll walk a few blocks to the Hungarian restaurant across from the Art Museum for dessert. There's an entire wall of cakes, pies, cookies, and tarts to choose from."

"When does the play start on Saturday?" Matt asked.

"Eight," Salvatore said. "I had the tickets held for pick up."

"Blacky and I will meet you at the theatre," Matt said. "She's going to help me find an apartment close to yours."

Detective Combs spoke again. "After this evening's meal, I'd like Stone to accompany me to her mother's apartment in Evanston to talk with the neighbors."

"I've already seen Salvatore's apartment building," Stone said to Grandma.

"Of course, dear," Grandma said. "Go help Mr. Combs. Your mother might have left some notations on a calendar or in her diary about her plans. I'll be praying for you."

"Not likely to help," Nosey said.

"Are you a praying man?" Combs asked Salvatore.

"Prayers always help." Salvatore smiled at Grandma, who did not return the politeness.

"Three months," Drape said out loud. "Sorry, Stone. I was thinking about how long it's been since you've seen your mother."

"Which church do you attend?" Grandma asked Salvatore. "We probably won't have time to attend services on Palm Sunday and catch the train back to Ann Arbor. Blacky and Matt are believers too. And, Nosey, don't you want to transfer your membership at St. Andrew's to an Episcopal church in Chicago?"

"No," Nosey said, putting her hand on Salvatore's knee. "I attended for social reasons and I think I'll be busy enough with my new job."

Salvatore stood. "Matt, I'll go buy you a newspaper in the bar for the latest apartment listings." He laughed. "Detective, I've been out of the field for a while, but I could introduce you to my precinct's captain. Would that help?"

"Immensely." Combs extended his hand to Salvatore. "I'm sure Stone would like to hear everything about her mother's relationship with you."

"He doesn't want to talk about Mother," Stone said.

Salvatore said, "The thing people least admire in me is my lack of gossip." He left the car to find a newspaper, after saying cryptically: "Talk among yourselves."

Combs spoke to Grandma. "I'll bring Stone back to Salvatore's apartment house Saturday morning. I'd like to look around her mother's old apartment there too."

"Stone," Grandma said. "I could stay with you at your mother's tonight."

Stone clapped her hands like a child. "That would be easier for me."

"Thank you, Mrs. Taylor," Combs said.

"Matt," Grandma said. "I promised Sky I wouldn't leave Drape's side. I want you and Blacky to guarantee me she won't be left alone."

"I'll be there," Nosey said.

Grandma smiled. "As you say, Nosey, you'll be busy enough."

* * *

Salvatore Bianco's Apartment Building
South Wabash and East Roosevelt

Drape wished Grandma had remained with them throughout the evening. Dinner was fine, but she was too nervous to eat much. Nosey dominated the conversation, asking Salvatore a thousand questions about their new jobs at the Field Museum and details about his apartment building, all of which he hardly answered. Drape was constantly aware of Salvatore's fixation on her.

Nosey finally stopped her dinner interrogation, pouting in anger.

Detective Combs, Stone, and Grandma said their goodbyes. Grandma didn't add any cautions to her goodbye, but she did pinch Drape's arm, a signal to pay attention.

Matt insisted all three girls share the sleeping arrangements in the top floor apartment in Salvatore's brick building. "I'll come back in the morning to help choose which apartment you might like best, Blacky."

"Why don't you stay with Salvatore?" Blacky asked.

Matt shook his head, "I think Combs wants to pick my brains about Stone's relationship with her mother. Stone and Drape's grandmother will be at the apartment. Combs and I are staying at the Hilton in Evanston. Nosey, do you mind if I pray with you three before I leave?"

"No harm, no foul." Nosey plopped down on the couch.

Matt extended his hands to Drape and Blacky. "May the sun bring you new energy every day. May the moon softly restore you by night. May the water wash away your worries. May the wind blow new strength into your being. May the earth rebalance you as you walk through the world. May you see yourself in all things bringing peace to all of God's creation."

* * *

Saturday, March 23

Salvatore Bianco's Apartment House

In the morning, Grandma and Stone knocked on the apartment door. Drape had slept on the couch. She could hear someone starting to stir in the bedroom.

"A Jewish breakfast for all!" Grandma set several bags of take-out from a nearby deli on the dining-nook's table.

Stone seemed cheered up. "Your grandmother makes me laugh. Detective Combs said he found enough evidence too."

Grandma tipped her head, waiting for Stone to explain more for Drape.

"He thinks Mother's been murdered too," Stone said.

"Murdered?" Drape asked. Drape hadn't taken her seriously when they visited the Henderson's and Grandma had mentioned the force of winning truth. She had hoped Matt's comment about swift justice had put Stone's fears at rest. Did her young friend need psychiatric help? "Have you been thinking all these three months your mother has been murdered?"

"I did." Stone opened several cupboard doors, selecting plates for their breakfast. "I couldn't keep repeating how I felt, or you would have thought my poor mind had taken a wrong turn. But I knew."

"It's the shock," Grandma whispered. "Detective Combs says Stone is being very brave. He thinks he will find her mother's killer."

Drape sat down at the table. She needed to bathe and wash her hair, but she could hear one of the girls in the shower. "Combs said he wanted to see Salvatore's—I mean your mother's apartment here too."

"Matt's bringing him," Grandma said. "Are we going to visit where the girls will be working too?"

"We are." Drape wished Sky had come. Too much was happening on this trip. She whispered to her grandmother, "Nosey's mad at me."

"I can understand why." Grandma folded the deli's napkins into triangles. "Nosey's in love with a man too old for her, who happens to be besotted with you."

"You don't know that." Drape wanted it *not* to be true. She needed to keep Salvatore as a friend. He understood her, didn't he? "He knows I'm marrying Sky."

"Yes, he does," Nosey said, coming in from the hall. She was dressed in her running garb. "And you'll be leaving Chicago soon."

51

"Nosey," Drape began, but didn't know what to say. "You're important to me. I'm going to miss you in Ann Arbor."

Nosey stood still for a moment before entering the bedroom. "I'll miss our days in Ann Arbor too." She didn't turn toward them. "The streets seemed safer to run on."

But Nosey wouldn't miss Drape's absence from the vicinity of Salvatore. Drape could fill in the unsaid implications. For a moment Drape thought she could almost summon up Salvatore's exotic scent.

Matt and Combs arrived before Nosey escaped into the bedroom.

Matt said to Nosey, "We saw you jogging down the alley, when we drove around the corner. Maybe you should take Blacky with you next time."

Blacky entered the eating area from the bedroom. Her newly washed hair hung in curly ringlets around her shoulders. "Where were you?" she asked Nosey.

"Running," Nosey said. "What else?"

Blacky didn't seem satisfied, but Matt embraced her. "I'm at the end of the block. I mean, I found an apartment and Mr. Combs has a lead on a job opening at a local limo service."

"Eat, eat!" Grandma said. "Then we can tour this apartment house in the daylight. Nosey, do you like the top floor?"

"I do." Nosey picked up a salted bagel. "I'll be able to see bird nests in the trees this spring."

Blacky still held Matt's hand after they were seated at the table. "What floor is your apartment on?"

"The second. It's not wise for women to take a first floor apartment."

"I agree," Grandma said as she loaded up everyone's plates with bagels, cream cheese, sliced tomatoes, onions and smoked salmon. "Drape, hurry take your shower, we want to survey the place before Salvatore gets here."

"Why is that?" Nosey asked.

"We wouldn't want to hurt his feelings if we say anything against his property," Grandma said. "Don't you agree?"

Nosey nodded as she rushed into the bathroom, beating Drape to the shower.

Blacky followed Drape into the bedroom, knocking on the bathroom door. "Nosey, what time did you leave?"

"Why?" Nosey called from under the shower.

"You weren't in your bed when I woke up last night." Blacky was wringing her hands.

"Must have made a trip to the bathroom," Nosey called in answer.

Blacky shook her head "no" to Drape. Drape opened her hands to gesture she had no idea what was going on. Blacky whispered, "Salvatore."

Drape pointed to the bathroom and Blacky acknowledged she meant Nosey had been with Salvatore the night before, alone.

"Nosey?" Drape started to come right out and ask her, but Nosey pushed past her.

"Better hurry if you want to see all the apartments." Nosey dressed quickly.

Drape shrugged her shoulders at Blacky. "Before I step into the shower, Blacky, is there a Bible here?"

Blacky opened the bedside table. "Just like a hotel. Here's a Gideon."

"Good enough," Drape sat down on the bed. *Please, Lord, what is your will?* She read Proverbs 3:5 to herself: "Trust in the Lord with all thy heart; and lean not unto thine own understanding."

Grandma had a breakfast plate and a coffee ready when Drape reemerged into the crowded front room. Of course in front of everybody, Blacky hadn't brought up the subject of Nosey's whereabouts during the night.

Detective Combs was the first to finish breakfast. "Did Salvatore leave keys with you, Nosey?"

"He gave them to Blacky," Nosey said.

"Oh, Matt, come help me look."

"Matt, you stay where you are," Grandma said and then shrugged at Drape. "Oh, go ahead, don't dawdle."

Drape wondered if Blacky would tell Matt about Nosey's excursion last night, but Matt seemed relaxed when they came back from the bedroom, a sure sign Blacky hadn't worried him. Blacky shook her head, meaning not to discuss Nosey's indiscretion. "Matt's going to show me his apartment. We'll meet you at the theatre."

Then the crowd toured the four apartments, which were arranged around a common garden.

Each floor's layout contained four narrow rooms-- a living room opening to the front halls, bedroom, large bathroom, and a kitchen eating area with access to the center courtyard, where they could see the tops of crocus popping up through a slight covering of snow.

"Built in the early forties," Grandma said.

CHAPTER FIVE

The first to enter the apartment's basement storage area, Drape smelled Salvatore's cologne, or at least the exotic scent she associated with him. "What is that odor?"

"I smell it too," Detective Combs answered. "Is it formaldehyde?"

"No that's stronger," Drape said. "Maybe Salvatore has stored some of his work clothes from the museum here."

Combs made a note on his cell phone. "I wonder if I need a search warrant to go through these boxes."

Towering over them on the basement steps, Salvatore abruptly appeared behind Grandma, Stone, and Nosey. "Oh, go ahead, Combs. Nothing to hide. Could Mrs. Slager have left some of her belongings behind?"

"Stone, do you recognize anything of your mother's?" Combs said, already opening a box. "Could I have your keys for these other cages?"

"Sure, sure," Salvatore said. "I think the owners who left all this stuff wouldn't mind your searching for a murderer's identity. My workshop is open too."

As they walked into the windowless basement shop, the smell Drape associated with Salvatore was even stronger. "Is that glue I smell?" she asked Salvatore.

"I don't think so. Could be from the oil on my tools." Salvatore said. "Something always needs fixing when you own an apartment. Tenants think landlords are all magicians."

"It helps to be a jack-of-all trades," Nosey said.

Salvatore spent a half-hour giving Nosey and Combs a tour of his saws, drills and presses.

Drape wandered into the darkest part of the workroom, where the smell was the strongest. Lined against the concrete-block wall were wooden packing crates. "Salvatore," she called. "Professor Carrington could use some of these boxes to ship specimens to other museums."

Salvatore was at her side. His arm brushed her shoulder as he opened the lid of one of the four feet by four feet wooden caskets with a small crowbar. "He's already ordered six. Professor Foster says he looked into the U of M museum security and won't need my help. Seems the job is under the Campus Police jurisdiction in Ann Arbor, but they are going to beef-up their security sweeps. I explained the Field Museum used my shipping crates."

"You make these here, then?" Combs asked.

"Oh, Drape," Salvatore said, moving too close again. "You probably smell the resin I use on the outside to make them almost waterproof."

Drape stepped aside trying to keep away from Salvatore and within Nosey's view.

Nosey had her back to them and was explaining the process to Grandma. "The specimens do need to stay dry for long periods of time."

Combs examined the inside of three of the boxes after asking Salvatore for his crowbar.

Drape wished she could smell Sky's clean Irish Spring soap right about now. Salvatore's closeness, the smell of the resin, or Salvatore's low voice began sending electrical charges up her arms and neck. Was it fear or attraction? If Grandma, Stone, Nosey, and Combs hadn't been a few feet away, Drape thought she might run screaming from the room. *Lord,* she prayed, trying to calm down, *Is my worry about Stone's mother or my upcoming wedding making me so crazy?*

"Creepy," Grandma said, once they'd exited the workroom.

Combs asked Salvatore, "Don't you get high on the fumes?"

"I must be accustomed to the smell. You know, Drape." Salvatore steadied her arm as they walked up the steps, placing his hand under her elbow, too close to her side. "You can only distinguish the differences in scents at a perfume counter for a few minutes."

"That's true." Drape took a step up, toward Combs.

Nosey's frown was becoming permanent.

Salvatore seemed to notice. "Nosey, did you want to show the girls where you will be working too?"

Nosey nodded. "We'll catch the bus out front."

"I would like a tour, Nosey," Drape said, hoping Salvatore wouldn't need to accompany them.

Drape approved of the closeness of the bus stop to the apartment's front entranceway. The street was busy enough because of the shops on the first floor of Salvatore's apartment building. An artists' café, burger house, and what looked like a restaurant bar next door invited clientele who would have passed any college campus dress code.

Nevertheless, as soon as they got down from the bus, the strong winds off Lake Michigan swirled the snow around them, giant flakes hitting them horizontally instead of politely falling. Salvatore said Grandma needn't brave the cold. So, Grandma and Salvatore boarded the next bus with Stone and Combs for the five-block ride back to the apartment.

Drape only made positive comments to Nosey, but Salvatore was right: the Field Museum's working rooms were *not* as elegant as the University of Michigan's Zoology and Paleontology Departments' halls. Nosey showed Drape where Blacky and she would be helping students in the laboratories.

* * *

After dinner in a Mexican restaurant, Grandma, Stone, and Combs climbed into one taxi for the short ride to the Goodman theatre. In the taxi Drape boarded, Salvatore got in last. Nosey was in the middle and Drape moved closer to the door to give them room. Nosey hiked up her skirt, crossing her bare legs for Salvatore's benefit. Drape felt like tugging down Nosey's hemline but decided the act mimicked Grandma's actions too closely.

Matt and Blacky did show up for the theatre and Matt insisted Drape sit between Blacky and Nosey. "You'll all be separated soon enough."

Grandma, Stone, and Combs sat across the aisle from the five of them.

Salvatore was sitting next to Nosey and reached across her to comment on the play to Drape several times. "Here comes the bed trick," he said at one point.

In response, Drape whispered to Nosey, "I know. I read the play."

But Salvatore continued to disregard Nosey and speak directly to Drape. Why was Nosey even attracted to this older man, who seemed to ignore her existence? Had Nosey's father abandoned the family home? Drape understood her own reaction to Salvatore's flattery might be triggered by the void in her own life. The negatives surrounding a sperm-bank donor and the resulting lack of a father figure in her home left Drape too vulnerable to older males. But surely Nosey's traditional parentage had provided her with the normal amount of love and support?

By the end of the evening Drape wasn't sure Nosey was even her friend.

Mimicking the sleeping arrangements of the night before, Stone went to Evanston with Grandma, and Matt and Combs stayed at a hotel in Evanston too. Salvatore said goodnight and Drape, Blacky and Nosey went up to the top-floor apartment.

"I'll sleep on the couch," Nosey said.

Drape thought it might be a peace offering, but Blacky looked suspicious. "I don't think you'll have time for a morning run before we leave for the train."

"I hadn't planned to run," Nosey said.

Ice seemed to have seeped through the windows. Drape approached Nosey. "I know you're angry, Nosey, but Salvatore only made comments to me to compare the production to the written play."

Nosey shook her head. "Right. Why didn't you talk to me about the play?"

"I did," Drape said but couldn't recall much of a conversation. "Remember, I told you they didn't behead the drunkard."

"Stupid play," Nosey said. "In *Tosca* more people die."

"I like happy endings," Drape said. Nosey walked away still angry.

"Of course," Blacky said. "You didn't mention the real cause of your disagreement."

Drape knew she was right. Salvatore paid rapt attention to every move and word of Drape's. Drape laughed to cover her embarrassment. Even Sky didn't constantly gaze at her as if she might melt before his eyes. She did not confide to either of her friends that under Salvatore's constant scrutiny, her obsession with Sky's future—their time ahead together—was ebbing slightly.

* * *

Palm Sunday, March 24
Train back to Ann Arbor

Grandma started napping in the sun's warmth as soon as the train moved out of the Chicago station. Stone sat next to her. She smiled at Drape, acknowledging her companion wouldn't be much of a conversationalist. Nosey, Blacky and Matt stayed in Chicago to buy furniture for their apartments.

Detective Combs sat next to Drape. He was shorter than Salvatore and probably closer to Sky's age. Slightly balding, his jeans, sweater and leather jacket let him blend into any crowd. Grandma had waved to him before Drape recognized the detective as he approached them at the crowded station.

Combs spoke softly so as not to wake Grandma. "Salvatore will be spending time at the Evanston police station. The apartment management made copies of their surveillance tapes. He'll call us if they find anything. He's checking with travel companies in the area too."

"You've brought my mother's computer with you?" Stone asked.

"I trust some of the geeks at the university will help me find any deleted material on her hard drive," Combs said. "We're lucky Salvatore has time to spend on the investigation."

"Will there be a memorial service in Chicago?" Drape asked.

"No. Mother was an only child too. We don't have family."

"You are holding up marvelously," Combs said.

Stone seemed to chew on the compliment. "Usually, when people describe me to others, they concentrate on Mother's unhappiness. I understand my personality isn't ebullient enough."

Drape looked at Combs, who seemed at a loss for words too. Drape wished Grandma had stayed awake long enough to come up with an appropriate comment. "Your mother's unhappiness wasn't caused by you," Drape said. "You couldn't control her feelings or cure them."

Combs studied Drape. "That's an Al-Anon saying."

"Is it?" Stone asked. "It is very comforting."

Grandma opened one eye and winked at Drape.

* * *

Rohn Federbush

Sigma Kappa House

Ike opened the sorority's door for the four of them. "The wedding and shower invitations are all mailed."

Mrs. Mack fluttered around Grandma. "Have you eaten? Would you like a cup of tea?"

Grandma waltzed into the sitting room as if she'd always lived amongst them. "Coffee would be heavenly."

Stone hurried off to her sanctuary.

Drape understood staying with people for hours without recharging her energy through solitude left Stone edgy.

"Did I say something wrong?" Detective Combs asked Mrs. Mack when she reappeared with a teacart filled with sandwiches, cakes, tea and coffee.

Mrs. Mack smiled. "Stone will be down for the evening meal. We are quite accustomed to our Stone needing time alone."

"April Fools," Ike said.

Drape sighed. "You mean the invitations aren't mailed."

Ike laughed wickedly. "No, I mean I fooled you just by saying April Fools. Of course, I mailed out everything. We worked like dogs."

"Don't exaggerate, Ike," Mrs. Mack said. "Besides, I enjoyed adding notes to all your sorority sisters.

Ike rolled her eyes behind Mrs. Mack's back and Drape got the picture. They'd spent an inordinate amount of time on the invitations. Drape made a praying symbol with her hands. "Thank you both. I'll make it up to you."

"Tell us about the apartments," Mrs. Mack said, after serving everyone and choosing her favorite cookie to go with apricot tea.

Grandma perked up. "Red brick with lead latticed roll-out windows. Lots of trees and a private courtyard for flowers. There were crocus and the tops of daffodil greens already coming up. Very nice really. Nosey has the top floor and Blacky is on the second, because Matt is on the second floor of an apartment down the block. Aren't children funny?"

Mrs. Mack nodded.

Ike wrinkled her nose. "Salvatore lives where?"

"Oh, we don't know, do we, Drape?" Grandma admitted.

Combs sat up straight, sloshing tea onto his indestructible jeans. "He has a wood-working shop in the basement."

60

"The better to cut up bodies," Ike laughed, but no one joined in.

"Pristine," Grandma said, but she wasn't drinking her tea. "No windows in the place."

"No windows in the apartment?" Mrs. Mack set her emptied cup on the tea cart. "I thought you said they were latticed."

"None in the basement." For some reason Drape thought of the shipping boxes.

"When you went to the Chicago Precinct, did they explain why Salvatore left?" Grandma asked. "Isn't he too young to retire?"

"We did go, but his friends weren't on duty." Combs took out his phone to tap in more notes. "He's helping with the investigation in Evanston." Ike tipped her head and Combs stood up. "I'll just be going along, Mrs. Mack. I need to have Mrs. Slager's hard drive analyzed."

When they heard the front door close, Ike poured herself another cup of tea. "The trouble with believers is you are all too trusting, don't you think?"

"Belief in the Lord has nothing to do with our lack of attention to a few details," Drape said. "Salvatore kept us very busy."

"I bet he did," Ike hooted. "Grandma, you probably were too tired to stay with Drape all the time."

"Well, you're wrong there!" Drape's nerves caused her to rattle her teacup in its saucer. She set it down on the magazine table next to the couch. "Matt or Grandma were with us all the time."

"I didn't like him cozying up to you in the basement," Grandma stirred another spoonful of sugar into her tea. "But I think you should stay here at the sorority until graduation. Your mother has made another reservation for me at the hotel."

"I didn't like Salvatore touching me either," Drape admitted. "The man drives me crazy. I don't know if I'm afraid of him or attracted to his animal magnetism."

"No such thing," Ike said.

Mrs. Mack and Grandma nodded their heads and said in unison, "Oh yes, there is."

"We should pray for him," Mrs. Mack said. "Let me bring in more hot water for the tea." She scurried off toward the kitchen.

"We could thank the Lord for loving him," Drape said. "Salvatore says he's a believer."

"And you believe him, don't you?" Ike said.

"I appreciate your honesty and Sky's." Drape let Mrs. Mack heat up her cup with hotter tea. "It shows a high degree of integrity to admit you can't conform to a widely held belief."

"The Bible says we need to accept faith." Mrs. Mack offered Ike a refill too. "Ike, I'm not the one to convince you, but I pray someone else will. Don't get angry with us."

Ike smiled then. "I know you love me and want the best for me."

Drape wanted to quote Proverbs 3:11 out loud: "Despise not the chastening of the Lord; neither be weary of his correction." But offending Ike was not going to bring her closer to belief.

* * *

Saturday, April 13
Briarwood Bridal Shop

The fashion consultant brought out more chairs for Drape and her friends. "My name is Daphne. Just call me when I can show you more dresses."

The mirrored room was lined with racks of wedding gowns, bridesmaid dresses and mother-of-the bride outfits. Even Nosey seemed cheerful as she helped Stone tuck her hair under a paisley scarf to hide its disarray. Mother and Grandma were all smiles. Drape insisted Mrs. Mack be a part of the group too. Drape realized her big day was important to them too. Mother hadn't had a wedding for Grandma to plan.

Ike and Blacky were busy arguing over bridesmaid dresses. "I can't wear pink," Blacky was saying. "Look at my hair."

Drape envied Blacky's curly red hair. Her own was an un-remarkable brown. Perhaps her birthplace in Tampa explained the sun-caught radiance of Blacky's soft and shiny hair. Of course, Blacky would be the first to decide on a dress. Dyslexic Blacky's problem-solving outshone them all. Drape understood Matt didn't have a clue why this beauty allowed him to squire her around. If one needed one word to describe a person, *focused* would say it all for Blacky.

"Well I disappear in green," Ike said.

With a bushel on her head, Ike would never go unnoticed. Her height didn't explain the phenomenon. The way she carried her regal head deterred the faint-hearted from approaching, and Ike was not shy about pointing out inconsistencies if not downright failures in those around her. Drape knew her not to be the callous person others might deem her, but there were times Drape wished Ike had sought more positive or encouraging words to explain the truth she spoke.

Stone said. "I hope we don't all decide to wear black. Weddings shouldn't be decorated as funerals. Love should be celebrated with lights and rainbows. We could all wear different colors."

"Excellent solution," Daphne said. "Would you like long gowns or short?"

"Short," Mother said. "These young things have beautiful legs."

"Easier to add to their wardrobes, after the wedding," Grandma agreed.

Drape was afraid she'd waste time trying on fifteen dresses. The verse from Proverbs 4:9 she'd read spurred her on: "[Wisdom] shall give to thine head an ornament of grace, a crown of glory shall she deliver to thee. "We need to decide quickly. We have final exams to study for this week."

Daphne approached. "Why don't you all select your dresses while I help Miss Taylor choose a few to try on?"

The wedding would be colorful. Mother chose a bright blue suit. Grandma's was pink and Mrs. Mack settled for a pale green. The bridesmaid dresses had straight skirts, a sleeveless bodice decorated with seed-pearl loops around the neckline. Blacky's dress was an emerald green, Nosey's a pale purple, Ike's was light blue, and Stone insisted on yellow.

The first satin dress Daphne chose enhanced Drape's slim hips. "But I want to resemble a southern belle from the Civil War."

A full-skirted creation Drape decided to don was crinkled in the latest style. "You look like a pillow," Grandma said, discouraging the choice.

The neckline on another dipped to the waist. "No," Nosey said. The lace-trimmed neck on the next scratched Drape's throat.

Grandma moved Daphne away from the girls, but Drape was close enough to hear. "Let Drape make a sketch for you."

Daphne provided the paper and Drape penciled her own concept. The skirt was full. The short-sleeved bodice was modest enough to show a hint of cleavage.

Ike hung over her shoulder. "Add lines of sewn-on pearls at the waist and hem."

"Do you need a ruffle on the bottom?" Stone asked.

"No," Blacky and Nosey said together and then giggled.

"Perfect," Daphne said. "We'll need you to come in for a fitting in a week." The veil selection used up another hour, but Daphne complimented them: "You all are the most efficient group of shoppers I've ever dealt with."

* * *

Sunday, May 5
Sigma Kappa Sorority

Sky was thankful Salvatore was not in the sorority house when he arrived with Drape, Grandma and Mother Taylor. Drape's cap and gown had been delivered to the sorority, and Drape insisted they arrive early. Graduation day had all the girls in a flutter, except for Stone.

She was the first to join him in the living room. "Drape will be down shortly."

"I'm sorry to hear about your loss, Stone," Sky stood up until Stone sat down. Her graduation hat tipped toward her nose. When she removed it, they tried not to comment on her hair.

Stone ran her hand over the short stubble. "Made a mess of it, didn't I?"

"Have the girls seen it?" Mother Taylor asked.

"Mrs. Mack said we'd fix it tomorrow." Stone plopped her mortarboard back on her nearly bald head. "My hair gets so tangled and I hate it when the brush pulls on my scalp. It's painful. So I just grabbed the scissors. No one's interested in how I look anyway."

"Hair grows fast enough," Grandma said.

Sky ruffled his, thankful for each lock.

"Did you see that mess?" Nosey walked in. "On today of all days."

Mrs. Mack followed on Nosey's heels, flapping her hands to resemble the mother hen she was to the girls. "No one will notice, Stone. Everyone will be too busy with their own business." She frowned at Nosey, who slapped the back of Stone's head.

"You need to be presentable to apply for a job, idiot." Nosey would brook no nonsense.

Mrs. Mack clapped her hands. "Nosey, you will apologize. Stone, you have enough to deal with. My hairdresser has fixed many a disaster from my charges over the years."

"This bad?" Stone asked.

"Once." Mrs. Mack struggled not to laugh. "A redhead attempted to dye her hair black by herself, and it fell out in clumps!"

Grandma said, "That's a lot worse."

Ike and Blacky entered, both shaking their heads. Ike said, "I wish I could offer a hair transplant."

Blacky leaned over to straighten Stone's cap. "Here, I brought you my favorite screw earrings."

"You'll be elegant." Mother Taylor offered a rare smile.

Sky admitted the earrings did help the situation, if only to fool Stone into thinking she looked better. Finally Drape arrived. He slipped his hands under her unzipped graduation robe to hold his bride-to-be close for a second or two. "Here you are." He whispered, "You're the best in the show."

"Flatterer!" Drape batted at his hands.

Sky didn't add that he was glad Salvatore Bianco was absent. "My folks have their tickets too."

"What time is it?" Ike asked. "Nosey, when are you and Blacky leaving for Chicago?"

Blacky answered by going over to Mrs. Mack and hugging her. "Right after the ceremony. Matt's driving us all the way in a van his employer sold to him for a hundred dollars. They told him it was his severance package. Its book value is over $15,000."

Mrs. Mack patted Matt on the shoulder. "People value you."

"We'll be back for the shower," Nosey nodded to Drape, who applauded as though she were surprised.

"Time to go," Matt said as he opened the sorority's door. "The van awaits."

* * *

At the door, they ceased laughing and elbowing each other because Salvatore Bianco walked up the sidewalk holding a stack of presents. "Congratulations," he said directly to Drape.

Mrs. Mack stopped in her tracks. "Salvatore, do you have a ticket for the ceremony?"

65

"I do," Salvatore said. "Nosey invited me."

Drape thought Sky might punch Nosey, or someone. He guided Drape toward her mother and grandmother.

Drape's stomach dropped. Nosey, Blacky and Matt would be gone after today, out of her Ann Arbor life. Wasn't today's verse, Proverbs 4:11, meant to guide her? "I have taught thee in the way of wisdom; I have led thee in right paths." She held out her hand toward Sky. "I'm ready," she said, taking a backward glance at Salvatore, who looked broken-hearted. Didn't he?

Chapter Six

Saturday, May 11
Sigma Kappa Sorority

In the middle of the wedding shower, Drape realized she hadn't seen Nosey Peterson arrive. At least fifty brightly colored gift boxes were stacked on the dining room table vying with Mrs. Mack's buffet offerings. Mrs. Mack explained that the sorority sisters unable to attend sent presents too.

Dressed casually in slacks and a lace top, Ike was passing out pens and card stock for an Advice for the Newlyweds game. Sentences in the puzzle started with the first letters of Cosmos Henderson's and Curtain Taylor's names.

Professor Chinich sat next to Grandma on one of the living room couches. "Who is Cosmos?" he asked, "the father?" Grandma laughed and Chinich put his arm around the back of couch where Grandma was sitting, to better scrutinize her game card.

"Sky's real name is Cosmos," Grandma explained, smiling much too long at Sky's old professor.

Drape was standing with her back to the fireplace, searching for a glimpse of Nosey. Proverbs 4:23 rang in her ears. "Keep thy heart with all diligence; for out of it are the issues of life."

Matt and Blacky joined her. "What's another word for *everybody*?" Matt asked as he endeavored to fill out the second 'e' on his card.

"Eventually," Blacky said. "Drape, it's a lovely party. I love you in that coral rose dress. But you don't look like you're having a good time. Are you worried about something?"

"Didn't Nosey come with you and Matt from Chicago?"

Blacky shook her head and whispered, "She told me Salvatore would bring her. She was acting a bit strange last night. She said she had a 'plenty big' surprise for me and asked for my key. I think she meant to give me a house-warming gift."

Matt scowled. "A present requiring your key?"

"You went shopping together." Drape meant to solve the mystery. "Did you *ooh* and *ah* over some lamp. Maybe Nosey decided to give to you."

"I don't remember." Blacky swiped at Matt's arm. "You know I trust her."

"She never admitted to sleeping with Salvatore," Matt was rude enough to point out.

Blacky kissed him and then said, "I stayed all night at Matt's, because I trust Matt too."

Drape shushed them. "Sky and I are in the same house, and Grandma does sleep a lot. The trouble is our morals won't let us haphazardly use each other. You trusted Nosey enough to give her your key, but where is she?" Chagrined at her lack of hostess skills, Drape smiled at the couple. "We'll find her. Matt, go eat more of Mrs. Mack's food or her feelings will be hurt."

Drape then headed toward Detective Combs, who was sitting on the steps to the sorority's upstairs. He was helping Stone fill out the game's sentences. "Have you seen Nosey come in?" Drape pointed to the open front door.

"We might not have noticed." Stone did not raise her head as she concentrated on the game.

Combs said, "My computer wizards at the university restored Mrs. Slager's emails on her hard drive. Salvatore Bianco threatened her to make her date him on New Year's Eve."

"What kind of threat?" Drape asked.

Stone interrupted, "He could have been kidding. He said she hadn't seen a dermestid colony box."

"Why would your mother want to see the university's dermestid box?" Drape wasn't interested in Salvatore's tomfoolery. "Stone, was she planning to visit you in Ann Arbor?"

Stone shook her head and Combs concentrated on Stone's face.

Drape scooted past the couple, who were obviously falling in love, to go up a few steps to see if she could spy Nosey in the crowded rooms. To her left, Matt's father, Orlando North, was seated in the dining room's bay window diligently filling out his game card. Nearby, Mother Taylor and Geraldine Henderson were talking to Amanda Jenkins, the first African-American to join the sorority.

"What are you doing up there?" Ike scolded. "Come down and mingle."

"Nosey didn't come?" Drape asked, ready to cry. Suddenly, Combs stood up. Something in his alert manner frightened Drape. "What?" she asked.

"Wait until after the party." Ike stamped her foot.

Combs nodded. "Let's walk out back for a minute."

"Not yet," Ike said. She called to Mrs. Mack, "Has anyone finished the game yet?"

"Rose Grace has." Mrs. Mack motioned toward the woman. "Rose Grace Warner."

Professor Leland proffered his arm to the ancient sorority sister to escort her into the foyer. Professor Foster offered his arm too. Had either of them known Rose Grace while she attended the university? Professor Leland was old enough to have been a classmate. The elderly lady was dressed entirely in white and her regal stance inspired her escorts to straighten their backs.

Standing next to the staircase, two sorority sisters referred to the romantic moment. Graduating ten years earlier, their names were easy to remember because they resembled the Biblical sisters Mary and Martha. Mary Alice Walker told Margaret O'Malley, "The beat goes on."

Ike pulled Drape down from the steps and into the living room to stand next to Sky. "Now listen, everyone," Ike's voice rose to get their attention.

In her eighties, Marie Kerner was speaking loudly because either she or her audience was hard of hearing. Their mothers were probably Cary Grant fans. Judy Wlsnewski and Judy Hart were listening intently to a list of the changes in Ann Arbor's landscape since they'd left the sorority. "The bridge alone must have cost ..." Marie noticed everyone was staring and stopped mid-sentence. "Sorry."

Drape pasted a smile on her lips, after whispering to Sky. "Nosey isn't here." She barely listened to her guests' answers.

But Sky held up his hand. "Could you repeat that?"

Rose Grace raised her voice, "'N': Never go to bed angry."

Sky laughed. "I only heard, 'Never go to bed.'"

Sky's father slapped Professor Clarke on the back. "That's my son!"

Drape scooted away from Sky during the laughter that followed. Near the front room bay window, Salvatore was surrounded by a group of women: Mrs. Mack's guests about his age, Lucille Cohen, Gladys Jacobsen, and even Professor Jane Hazzard. They all joined Salvatore in chuckling at Sky.

Salvatore held out his arm to Drape, and she moved close to his side, stunned at how comfortable she felt near him. His arm supported her back, and his hand rested lightly on her hip. Here was the paternal aura she'd never been able to experience, safety and affection at her fingertips.

She stretched up and kissed the side of his cheek. "Blacky says you brought Nosey. Is she upstairs?"

Professor Hazzard moved between Drape and her view of Sky at the fireplace. Drape wasn't sure why she thought she needed to be aware of Sky's movements, but she was thankful to be blocked from his observation that she was standing this near to Salvatore Bianco.

Salvatore moved his hand from her hip to the middle of her back, pressing his fingertips to her backbone through her thin silk dress. "Nosey wasn't at the apartment when I went to pick her up. So I assumed Blacky and Matt had talked her into riding with them. I was about twenty minutes late." He bent down to add, with his breath close to her neck. "It was a lonely, long ride."

"She didn't come with them." Drape's face was close to his. His smell and the heat of his body tried to caution her. Salvatore's eyes seemed to bore into her soul. Drape stepped away, brushing past Professor Hazzard.

* * *

Sky was looking around trying to spot Drape. She raised her hand for him to see her and conversations ceased, so Drape took the opportunity to ask, "Does anyone know where Nosey Peterson is?"

Mrs. Mack held up her hand. "We'll figure it out later, Drape. It's time to open the presents."

Ike scowled. "I have another game."

Sky put his arm around Ike's shoulder. "Drape is upset about Nosey not coming. You've done a great job. Let's go unwrap the presents and let everyone go home."

Ike stepped away from him. "Mrs. Mack paid for all the decorations. Doesn't it look like a mad-crepe-paper fiesta?"

"Where in the world did she find all these lace umbrellas?" Sky counted at least twenty.

"She's not telling." Ike's laughter drew Drape's attention for a moment.

Drape's smile was getting rather rigid, by the time she'd plowed through the gaily wrapped boxes with Mrs. Mack and Mother Taylor listing each gift and donor for the thank-you note regime to follow.

Sky gravitated away from the lavish spectacle. Jake Carrington, about the same age as Combs, was rough-housing with him. Pushing and shoving Combs toward the sorority house kitchen. Sky followed them, thinking they must be kidding around, maybe searching for hard liquor to add to the insipid punch.

"I know a human bone from other mammals," Carrington was saying.

Combs had his head bowed bull fashion. Sky thought they were going to come to blows. "We need to have the police look at it." Combs must have heard Sky behind him. "Jake, you're the expert. You make the call."

Carrington nodded to Sky and walked out the back door.

Sky followed Combs outside. "What was that all about? Did Carrington find a human bone?"

"People get crazy when they hear a murder has touched someone they know." Combs scowled at Carrington's back. "He's dithering about, probably mixing up ape bones with human fossils. He says he's in love with Stone."

"Stone?" Sky didn't hide his surprise. "But she's ..."

"What?" Combs raised his voice. "She's what? Stone is a delicate, abandoned child. She has no family, now. Her mother never loved her." Combs wrung his hands.

Sky nodded. So Combs and Carrington were in love with Stone Slager. Spring certainly allowed every human's thinning blood to rush toward a mate. The sorority's back garden was ablaze in spring blossoms. Lilacs ruled the day, but lilies-of-the-valley, tulips, and hyacinths against a hedgerow of forsythia perfumed the air.

Even though he wanted to know where Carrington thought he found a human bone, Sky changed the subject to alleviate Combs' fit of jealousy. "What do we know about Nosey?"

"She's been seeing Salvatore Bianco," Combs said. "Matt seems to think she slept her way into the Field Museum job. And Nosey's closest friend, Blacky Schultz, doesn't defend her."

"When did they see her last?" Sky asked.

"I need to ask them, but I think it was two nights ago," Combs said. "I'm going to alert the Chicago and Evanston police departments. Salvatore said he retired from a precinct, but I haven't been able to confirm that."

Sky remembered Salvatore was supposed to be helping find Stone's mother. "Did he look at the Evanston apartment tapes for Stone's mother?"

Combs watched the backdoor of the sorority as if expecting Salvatore to arrive. "If he did, he hasn't told me he's found anything."

Blacky and Matt exited the house. "Salvatore's looking for you, Detective Combs."

"He wants us to go to Chicago with him to look for Nosey," Matt said.

"I know he's determined to find Stone's mother too," Blacky said. "I heard him tell Nosey that the last time he remembers laughing, Mrs. Slager lived in Nosey's apartment."

"That could mean anything," Sky said. "When did you last see Nosey?"

Further discussion was silenced when they noticed Stone Slager and Salvatore leaving through the back door. Salvatore was frowning and his hand on Stone's shoulder seemed to be causing her distress.

Combs started to run toward them but modified his gait. "Stone, what happened?" He pushed Salvatore away from her. "Stone doesn't like to be touched."

Salvatore's smile was chilling. "I was asking her who her mother might be with."

Stone stood behind Combs, facing away from all of them. "I asked him what he's done to our Nosey. Aren't these flowers lovely?"

Blacky let go of Matt's hand. "Salvatore, Nosey told me you were driving her to the shower."

As though the sun had suddenly warmed his bones, Salvatore's demeanor changed when he concentrated his charms in Blacky Schultz' direction. "Nosey was mistaken," he said. "I can't stand her wanton displays."

If he hadn't been so male, Sky could almost describe Salvatore's voice as sultry. Sky checked to see if Matt agreed.

Matt was grinding his teeth. He stepped in front of Blacky. "Combs is coming with us back to Chicago to find Nosey."

* * *

Detective Larry Combs admitted he didn't like men taller than himself. And Salvatore's shifting persona set him on edge. He wanted to ask if the real Salvatore Bianco would please step forward. He told the group in the yard. "Mrs. Mack needs us to keep our manners gracious while we tell her guests goodbye."

Stone touched his back. She so seldom made direct contact, he nearly gasped. Combs turned carefully not to startle her. So lovely. Her remaining hair, after she had lopped off most of it in desperation to comb it for graduation, was styled in a pixie cut. An expandable lace ribbon with a pink rosette crowned her cuteness. Her pug nose huge eyes behind her spectacles, and pouting mouth drove his body to distraction. And he daren't lay a finger on her, because her Asperger's caused an aversion to physical contact.

But Stone had cuddled up to him as they sat on the steps giving Drape and Sky silly wedding advice. The sheer material of Stone's dress's hem had brushed over the top of Combs' shoes. He reached down to move the pink stuff, lest it pick up any dust. Stone had rubbed the back of his hand with her fingertip, lighting timbers in his heart.

Combs smiled eye to eye with her. He could let her make the first moves. "What do you think, Stone?"

"We should make sure we don't upset Drape. Sky, she needn't be told we're going off to search for Nosey. She'll want to come too."

Sky *was* taller but such a quiet gentleman that Combs excused him from his prejudice against giants.

Sky said, "We do have an appointment with Pastor Nieman on Wednesday."

Combs said, "I'm your friend, Sky. Do this for me: keep Drape from coming to Chicago."

Sky nodded, "I'll see you inside. Better hurry before Drape misses all of us."

Salvatore reached out for Blacky's hand, but Matt stepped between them. "Mrs. Mack rules the day," Salvatore said, laughing lightheartedly.

Now Matt was the right size. Not as bright as his girlfriend or any of her sorority sisters, but Matt lived to serve. Although fifteen or sixteen years younger than Combs, something about his openness and courage to show his feelings toward Blacky let Combs trust the kid completely.

"Stone," Combs said, "pack a bag. You'll ride with Blacky and Matt." Stone reentered the house with Blacky and Matt close behind. "Salvatore?" Combs asked. "I hope you don't mind driving me back to Chicago?"

"Good time to talk about Mrs. Slager's Evanston tapes, right?" Salvatore said.

Combs hoped he was mistaken about a sly glint in Salvatore's blue eyes. It disappeared immediately when Combs stepped closer to check them out. Maybe he was an okay guy. Maybe it was only Salvatore's height and Stone's aversion to Salvatore's touch.

"Stone's kind of creepy," Salvatore said, shattering all of Combs' good will toward the man.

"Who asked you?" Combs hoped he could keep his temper in check on the long ride to Chicago. He smiled at Salvatore. Two could play this double game, if that was what they were doing, sparring around the issue of why all the women Salvatore Bianco knew—maybe even in the Biblical sense—conveniently disappeared from sight.

* * *

Sunday, May 12
Brighton Condo

Drape pretended she was asleep. She could hear Grandma moving the shower gifts around, but she wasn't prepared to face the day. None of the visiting sorority sisters planned to stay at Mrs. Mack's. Soon even Ike and Stone would move out.

They shouldn't have invited males to the shower. After the last guest left the party, all the men agreed to go crazy together. Grumbling and surly, Sky, Matt, Combs and even Salvatore bumped into each other, dropping presents as they carted them to Sky's van. It pretty much ruined any pleasant mood Drape might have conjured up if Nosey hadn't been missing.

Everyone seemed angry at Salvatore. In front of Grandma on the ride back to Brighton, Sky even said Salvatore told Blacky he never agreed to bring Nosey to Ann Arbor. Drape was sure that in the crowded bustle of the party, Sky had misunderstood. But no, he insisted Salvatore was caught in a lie.

"Then why did he agree to go back with Combs to look for Nosey?" Drape had asked. "Salvatore has been a father figure to all of us since we met him." Drape was sure she could reason Sky out of his hostile mood. "You know, just like the way Mrs. Mack mothers us."

"Matt told Combs that Nosey was Salvatore's lover before she got the job in Chicago." Sky's ears changed color as they did when he was embarrassed. "Sorry, Mother Taylor and Grandma. I need to warn Drape about his intentions."

Why Sky had found it necessary to malign Salvatore in front of Mother and Grandma was beyond her, so Drape changed the subject to needing a china cabinet for all the dishes she'd received at the wedding shower. Then she asked, "Weren't they supposed to buy personal items for me?"

"Not with all those men invited," Mother had said.

They'd taken Mother to her hotel, but Grandma stayed to chaperon Drape.

Drape rolled over to watch Grandma restack the presents. "Good morning."

"And to you." Grandma laughed. "Mercy, where are you going to store all these?"

"China cabinet," Drape said stretching away that last laziness of sleep. "Did you dream?"

"Make your bed, dear. We'll go shopping for flowers as soon as you've both had breakfast."

"Wasn't Sky crazy with jealousy last night?" Drape straightened the covers as directed.

Grandma watched. "I suspected Nosey was intimate with Salvatore."

"You didn't say anything." Drape sat down on the freshly made bed. "I don't believe it. He's so good to everyone. Blacky doesn't believe it, does she?"

"Didn't Sky say Matt told him?"

"He's just another jealous male." Drape was speaking aloud what she hoped in her heart. "Salvatore is too good looking. You saw how Mrs. Mack's friends mobbed him."

"And Professor Hazzard," Grandma said. "I'm not comfortable with his constantly touching you."

"He's harmless," Drape said, too quickly for even her own taste. Her reactions to his contact weren't the same as a daughter's would be to a father's affection, were they? "I don't know how I'm supposed to feel. Did your father hug you?"

"I kissed his cheek," Grandma said, "the way I saw you kiss Salvatore's yesterday."

Drape felt embarrassed. "Did Sky see me kiss Salvatore?"

"I don't think so."

"How did it feel to love your father? Was it the same as when you fell in love with your husband?"

Grandma laughed. "Pretty much. Richard was twenty years older. Of course, the marriage bed wasn't like getting tucked in at night by my father, which he didn't do anyway." Grandma sat down next to Drape. "You know what you feel, physically, when Salvatore is around. Are you being honest with yourself?"

Drape didn't want to think about Salvatore any more. Sky was waiting downstairs. "There are children who grew up without a father for other reasons."

Grandma nodded. "Even in the same family, one child is favored over another and that one might as well be orphaned."

Drape stood up. "Let's go out for breakfast. Anyway, Salvatore's back in Chicago for good. He didn't get the job he wanted at the Zoology Museum."

"Does Sky know he applied?"

"It didn't seem important," Drape said. Was she being scrupulously honest? At the time when Salvatore told her he'd interviewed for a position as a security guard, she was flattered because he'd wanted to stay near her.

And Salvatore wanted to work in the museum. He understood the old building's attraction to her. But maybe he didn't see her as a daughter he never had. Did that make a difference in their friendship? Salvatore never mentioned Sky. It was like he didn't believe she would actually marry him. Maybe that's how all fathers viewed their daughters' upcoming marriages. Maybe not.

It was Mother's fault.

Just because she couldn't find an efficient way of meeting a suitable husband, it didn't mean the short cut of a sperm bank was a good solution. Drape's imagination didn't fill in all the details of a relationship with a real, male, head-of-household. Would she even know if Sky was acting inappropriately toward his daughters ... the way Salvatore touched her lower backbone?

"Give me a moment," Drape said, reaching for her King James. "I'll be right down." "Lord, Forgive me for my sins known and unknown. Help me seek your truth, amen." In her King James version, Proverbs 4:24 read, "Put away from thee a forward mouth, and perverse lips put far from thee."

CHAPTER SEVEN

Salvatore Bianco's Lincoln
On the way to Chicago

Riding west on I94, Combs asked Salvatore about the Evanston tapes. "How many men visited Stone's mother in her new apartment?"

"No one," Salvatore said, keeping his attention on the stop-and-go traffic skirting Gary, Indiana. "I left the tapes with the Evanston police."

"No George?" Combs asked, remembering Salvatore had claimed Mrs. Slager's last encounter was named George.

"Not unless he was a UPS deliverer." Salvatore laughed.

Combs had to admit it was hard not to join in. He could see if he hadn't been in love with Stone, he might have given into Salvatore's infectious laughter. In love with Stone. There it was, the truth evident. And what was he going to do about it? Did Stone already suspect?

"I need to buy an engagement ring for Stone," Combs said, wanting to thwart any negative comments from Salvatore about Mrs. Slager or his intended.

Salvatore glanced his way for a second. "I didn't know."

Combs nodded, thinking, *Or you would have kept your mouth shut about thinking Stone was creepy.* Would Salvatore be more secretive about his comings and goings now that he knew Combs' prejudice? Combs prayed his most comforting prayer: *Lord, aid me in discerning the truth, if it be your will.*

Probably to squash any such doubts about his veracity, Salvatore said. "The sorority sisters are probably closer to each other than blood relatives."

"I agree," Combs said, trying to salve any hard feelings. "When did you first meet Mrs. Slager?"

"Last summer," Salvatore answered immediately, perhaps to prove his willingness to be forthright. "I thought we had something permanent developing, but when Nosey arrived, Stone's mother wouldn't accept Nosey's romantic behavior as unsolicited."

"You were lovers," Combs said, ready to pass judgment on the twenty-year age difference.

Salvatore shrugged. "She thought I had influence at the Field Museum. All I did was introduce her to the woman in charge of Human Resources."

"But you were willing to act as guardian when Stone called you at the sorority house."

"I thought with more than one sorority sister in the vicinity, Nosey might straighten up. Stone's mother made it perfectly clear she was no longer interested in me. I think Nosey had talked to her."

"Then why did you follow Nosey to Ann Arbor in January?"

"That seems strange, I know. I was thinking that if Nosey and Blacky were working in Chicago with Matt around to check on them, I could avoid being around Nosey by getting a job in Ann Arbor. I showed up at the sorority and Mrs. Mack dragged me to Drape's condo. Now there is a beauty! Of course, Ike and Blacky are no slouches either."

What was Ike's description that Sky had shared with him? Then Combs remembered and repeated the gist of Ike's words, "So you're democratic with your admiration of young women?"

"As all men are. Isn't Stone ten years younger than you?"

Combs nodded at the counter point. "But Drape and Mrs. Mack are relying on you to be Nosey and Blacky's bodyguard in Chicago."

Salvatore laughed. "That's because Nosey didn't tell them how closely her body had commerce with mine."

"Once you were in Ann Arbor, did you get an interview at the museum?" Combs hoped their conversation didn't alert Salvatore to his methodical interrogation.

"Drape escorted me around, introduced me to her committee members." Salvatore shook his head. "I thought I made a good impression but ended up with only a purchase order for specimen shipping crates. Remember? You opened a few in my basement when you visited in March for the Shakespeare play."

"Stone and I missed the play. *Measure for Measure,* right?"

"That's it," Salvatore said. Something in his tone let Combs know the irony of the play's romantic shenanigans was not lost on Salvatore. Then Salvatore said in a lighter tone, "I'm hoping to make sure *all's well that ends well.*"

"That we find Mrs. Slager and Nosey?"

Salvatore flinched. Had he forgotten Combs was in the car, or the nature of their unhappy mission? "I'm sure we'll find where they went off to." Salvatore flashed his probably-rehearsed, reassuring smile.

Combs smiled back, not ready to show his skepticism. "When did you find out you hadn't been hired by the museum? Stone said you gave her a graduation present."

"I was still hopeful then. I thought Mrs. Mack would know the best way to find an income property like the one I own in Chicago for students. I'm still planning to sell Mother's old house in Chicago."

"I wondered why you came to Drape's shower."

"You're right, I wasn't invited. But Mrs. Mack insisted I stay when I presented myself. The girls always give me a warm welcome. I do like Ann Arbor's size better than Chicago's."

Not as knowledgeable of the city's streets as he was of Chicago's train connections, Combs was taken aback when Salvatore stopped in a residential neighborhood. They stopped in front of a huge, wraparound brick porch outside a small house. Matt, Stone, and Blacky were sitting on the wide concrete porch railing.

Combs ignored Salvatore as they got out of the car. "My mother's," Salvatore said apologetically. "You're welcome to stay the night."

Instead, Combs ran up the front steps. Stone moved down toward him.

Blacky walked over to Salvatore, who held out his arms expecting an embrace. Matt intervened. "Blacky can't find her key, so we've been waiting for you."

"Come inside." Salvatore made them feel right at home, directing Matt to the kitchen to make coffee for everyone. "We'll go out to eat as soon as I find an extra key."

"Nosey said she'd leave the key under the pot of geraniums," Blacky said. "We looked all over the entrance. No key under any pot."

Combs struggled to stay tuned-in to what was happening around him, but Stone consumed every fiber of his attention. Her hair had grown a bit, or else the long ride had encouraged her short hair to curl into unruly bunches.

"I'm cold," Stone said. Combs couldn't have ripped his coat off any faster if a charging bull had headed right for them. He tenderly draped her shoulders. She smiled at him. "I'm not made of china."

Combs kept one hand on her forearm, not yet sure how much he was allowed to show his affection. "I want to hold you to my chest."

"I'd like that," Stone said.

Gently he folded her in his arms and noticed her shivering might not be blamed on the chilly evening. "You own my heart," he said.

Matt tapped his shoulder. "You're welcome to stay the night with me. Blacky and Nosey's apartment house is only a block away if we walk through the alley."

"Really?" Combs said, trying to remember why that was important news. "Where's Salvatore?"

Blacky pointed to a basement entrance in the kitchen. "He's looking for another key."

"Stay here," Combs said to Stone. He didn't know why, but he didn't want her following him into Salvatore's basement. Would there be another woodworking shop down there? As he reached the third step down, the fumes of the basement reached him. He smelled the odor Drape had commented on when they visited Salvatore's basement workshop in the girls' building. Salvatore had explained it as resin, but it smelled more rancid than a chemical normally could.

"Come on down," Salvatore called.

* * *

Sigma Kappa Sorority House

"Rackham's Graduate Admissions Director, Nan Purdue, is a sorority sister too," Mrs. Mack said, brushing crumbs off her pristine lap.

Drape knew the gesture signified a momentary embarrassment. "I'm sure our Stone made a good impression."

Mrs. Mack smiled her relief. "I spoke to Nan afterwards, and she said Stone couldn't have been more professional."

Ike was wheeling in the teacart and rolled her eyes at Mrs. Mack's last statement. "She'll do fine. She knows how to make young people relax."

Drape agreed. Stone's awkwardness was helpful in disarming the most nervous applicants. In comparison to Stone's inept social graces, most people felt better, if not a little superior. "I'm sure Stone is happy."

"How did you fare, Ike?" Sky asked as he accepted tea and a cake plate from her.

"This job search crap is for the birds. Sorry, Mrs. Mack. I sent in thirty applications, and only received three interviews."

"Isn't that a good percentage?" Drape asked. She hadn't needed to interview because Professor Foster offered her the permanent job teaching the class she had been substituting for old Professor Pollack. Neither Ike nor Stone wished to pursue a PhD. The competitive job market in Ann Arbor gave them little help, even with a Master's degree. PhDs without tenure were often seen in parking structure toll booths. Sky's family in Lansing's Mathematics Department greased his access to an Assistant Professor position, but it wasn't tenure track. Drape's would be, if she published enough papers.

"Good enough odds for me," Ike said. "Of course, being a friend to someone smart enough to include him on her thesis committee didn't hurt my chances with Professor Clarke."

Drape clapped her hands. "You'll love working with him. He's a real treasure."

"Now all we need to do is find apartments for you and Stone," Mrs. Mack said. She reached for a file folder on the end table next to Drape. "Over the years, I've collected quite of list of Ann Arbor landlords who have proven to be considerate and helpful when things go wrong."

"What could go wrong?" Ike laughed.

Mrs. Mack was dead serious. "Oh, plumbing and kitchen drains. You'd be shocked. But my list has reliable people." She patted the file folder in her lap.

Ike sat down next to Drape. "So, you know the landlord for the loft apartments in the old factory across the railroad tracks on Liberty?"

"No, dear," Mrs. Mack said. "That particular property was recently renovated by a Detroit-based owner."

Ike pinched Drape's thigh, where Mrs. Mack couldn't see her. "Too bad, I guess. I've ruined my life. I already signed a lease."

"Oh no," Mrs. Mack distressed. "Well if you need a lawyer in the future, I know a few who can get you out of the lease."

Drape could have kicked Ike for teasing Mrs. Mack. "Has Stone found an apartment?"

Mrs. Mack dusted off her shoulder as if anticipating too much praise. "You know my friend Larry Combs leases an apartment behind Border's old parking structure. I mean Old Borders parking structure. The parking structure is just fine. A friend of mine, really just an acquaintance, owns an apartment house right next door. That way, Stone will feel secure and Larry can keep an eye on her."

Sky whispered to Drape, "He'll probably want to keep his hands on her too."

Drape swiped at him and smiled at Mrs. Mack. "Sounds like you have everything under control. I'll see you at mass at St. Andrew's next Sunday for sure."

Proverbs 6:27 was worrying Drape. It caught in her throat, threaded its way through the gray matter under her skull, taunted her like an incessant melody: "Can a (woman) take fire into her bosom and her clothes not be burned?" Were thoughts of Salvatore overwhelming her good sense even if he was safely out of the city?

* * *

Henderson's Home in Lansing

"I didn't know Sky was a Gemini," Drape said.

Sky's father, Jim, took their coats. "You're Scorpio, November second, right?"

"I am," Drape said. "Mother wouldn't let me read anything about astrology. She said it was not science. Do I smell corned beef?"

Grandma seemed awfully pleased when Professor Clarke directed Chinich to help her with her coat. "Scorpio's love to talk." She smiled directly up into Professor Chinich's face. "Good enough reason to have a man in the house to sit with."

Chinich actually blushed at her attention. "I've lived alone all my life. Don't think I know how to live with another human being."

"You'll do fine," Professor Clarke said. "He's an excellent cook."

"Now that is unusual for a man of our generation," Grandma said.

Mother was getting steamed about something. "Good heavens, Mother, why don't you invite him down to Fort Lauderdale?"

Chinich offered Grandma his arm, and they preceded the rest of the guests into the brightly lit dining room. Drape was shocked to hear her grandmother whisper, "I do have three bedrooms."

Geraldine had arranged Sky's three-tiered birthday cake as the centerpiece. Her crystal was the same as their first dinner, but the plates were vintage bone china. "I'm so thankful Ike liked my dinnerware when she was here. I've been trying to find a home for it for years."

"You gave her the plates?" Jim asked.

"She wanted them."

"They were Sky's grandmother's," he said.

Geraldine's chin went up a notch. "I never liked them, but I thought the young people would be more comfortable visiting here for the first time without facing a table full of expensive china."

"You were very generous," Drape said. "They are collectors' favorites."

Sky interjected. "They'll fit with Ike's decorating scheme." Drape smiled, waiting for a further explanation. Sky noticed the silence too. "Oh, I helped her pick out a few pieces of furniture at IKEA when you all were in Chicago. Fits her name. You know, Drape, how Ike enjoys a good pun."

"I do," Drape smiled at him but wondered if Ike might have thoughts about racing her down the aisle to marry Sky.

* * *

Salvatore Bianco's Chicago Home

Combs was glad there were three young humans upstairs in the kitchen waiting for him. He approached Salvatore's shadow on the floor, but Salvatore startled him in the darkness behind him. He thrust a flashlight into Combs' hand.

Salvatore chuckled. "Did I scare you? The electricity is off down here for some reason."

Combs let the beam of light circle the room. In the far corner a large box emanated the reeking fumes. "What is that?"

"Dermestids," Salvatore explained. "They eat flesh off the museum specimens, right down to the bare bones. When I was younger, I skinned rare animals donated by big game hunters to the Field's Museum. Not many of them around anymore—big game hunters, I mean."

The odor was too fresh for Salvatore's story. "The girls are probably hungry," Combs said. "Should we pick you up after they get settled?"

"I think I'll pass," Salvatore said. "Bit tired after that long haul from Ann Arbor."

Combs followed Salvatore back upstairs, handed over the flashlight and then walked with Stone, Matt, and Blacky through the alley to Blacky's apartment house.

"I can't talk Blacky into giving up her job at the Field Museum," Matt said. "She'd be safer in Ann Arbor."

Blacky tossed her head, and the dim back-alley light sparkled in her strawberry-blonde hair. "I'd be homeless without a job. Does that sound safe to you?"

"You could live with me," Stone offered.

"Or we could marry," Matt said.

"Now there's an unromantic proposal if I ever heard one," Combs clapped Matt on the back.

"All in good time, Matt," Blacky said linking arms with him. "I need to prove myself. All those long hours of studying—not to mention my mountain of school loans—all demand I stay where I am."

"To avoid my pleadings," Matt said, kissing her for a second.

After they climbed the steps to Blacky's second-floor apartment, she unlocked the door. "Come on in. Matt, try to find something to quench our thirst. I think there's orange juice. I'm going to dump my bag in my room."

Stone hadn't moved from the front door. "This was Mother's apartment. Blacky has changed all the furniture."

"She wanted all new things," Matt said. "She couldn't stand the idea of someone else sitting on her couch or using her table."

Combs held out his hand for Stone, who hadn't moved from the open doorway. "I'm here. I'll keep you safe."

"I'm not afraid, just a little disoriented from the changes."

Combs rather liked the elegant mahogany pieces Blacky had chosen for the dining room area. The blue chintz fabric on the couch telegraphed that the young lady was in control of her environment.

Blacky burst back into the living room. "Matt!" Matt dropped the orange juice carton into the sink before leaping to her side. Blacky held him at arm's length. "Someone's been sleeping in my bed!"

CHAPTER EIGHT

Monday, May 13
Evanston

The next day, Stone and Combs packed up Mrs. Slager's belongings to ship them to the Ann Arbor address Mrs. Mack provided for the flat next door to Combs. Mrs. Slager's Christmas tree was still trimmed. Combs knocked on the neighbors' doors and invited Mrs. Slager's neighbors in to talk to Stone.

Stone's graciousness included giving away most of her mother's possessions. "We suspect foul play," she explained. "I haven't heard from her since Christmas."

Out of the five women and one man who attended the dismantling of Mrs. Slager's apartment, only two women, who seemed close to not remembering their own names, were rapacious in gathering up Mrs. Slager's belongings.

Another woman, and the man who seemed to be her partner, were the most distraught. He asked Combs, "What will she do, when you find her? You've given away all her possessions!"

Combs motioned for the man to join him in the kitchen. "I've been a detective for fifteen years now. Missing persons usually meet with violence if they haven't notified a family member of their whereabouts within three months' time."

"I'll explain what he said later," the older gentleman said to his partner. They settled on taking only a picture of Mrs. Slager and Stone taken in front of the Christmas tree. "You'll stay in touch, won't you?" the lady asked.

Stone assured them she would let them know whenever she heard anything.

After the remaining neighbor women had cleaned out Mrs. Slager's cupboards, refrigerator and closets, Stone was left to pack up the jewelry, linens, and the kitchen utensils. Combs arranged for the movers to clean the apartment when they left.

Then Stone and Combs headed for Evanston's police department. Combs unzipped his coat as they walked along Lake Michigan.

Stone lagged behind. "I'm sorry I'm so slow."

Combs offered his hand, which she grasped. "We're not exactly on a happy errand. I was rushing to get it over with, without thinking about how you must dread the investigation."

She sped up to keep pace with him. "I need to find answers."

"Winter's back is broken," Combs said to change the subject. "Not a bit of ice to be seen." Did she feel the same warmth spreading between them?

"I wish we could stand in the sun just to watch the waves break against the warm sand." She hadn't stopped walking, but Combs understood they shared the same communion of spirit.

"One of the sureties between us, Stone, is the love we both share for our Lord." Combs welcomed Stone's physical reply.

She linked arms with him. "He'll protect us."

After two hours of searching through the evidence room files, an Evanston uniformed officer handed Combs six tapes. "This is all the apartment manager sent us. Seems the tenant only lived there six months before she disappeared. Another private detective asked them to copy a set."

"Did they get his name?" Combs asked.

"Yep, right there." The officer pointed to the notation on the open-case file, 'Salvatore Bianco, Chicago detective.'"

In order not to break the chain of evidence, Combs sent Stone to search for coffee and sandwiches, while he set up a viewing monitor in an adjacent room in the police station.

Mrs. Slager's hallway and apartment entrance were both surveyed. Stone arrived with the provisions as Combs watched a woman unlock Mrs. Slager's door.

"That's Mother," Stone said. "I gave her the red scarf on her birthday."

Combs said. "The date on this tape is July fifteenth."

"Nosey and I visited her in Chicago on July fourth last year." Stone unwrapped their submarine sandwiches. "Do you want roast beef, or sliced salami? Mother must have moved immediately after we left."

"I'll take the salami. Was your mother upset with Nosey?"

"How did you know?" Stone asked. "I couldn't understand why, but Mother and I were rarely on the same page."

"Salvatore told me he was serious about your mother, until Nosey ruined it."

"Wasn't Salvatore too young?" Stone blushed. "Mother was twenty-five years older."

"I'm ten years your senior." Combs reached out his hand for her to hold.

Stone did better than that. She put her arms around his neck and kissed him on the mouth. "I love you, Larry. Don't you know that?"

"I was hoping," Combs said, not releasing her from his arms. "I told Salvatore I need to find you an engagement ring."

Stone moved away. "I bet he was surprised."

"Do you think he could have harmed your mother?"

"I know I don't read people as well as others, but he frightens me when he leers at Blacky and Drape. He never looked at Nosey in the same predatory way. So I never guessed anything was going on between them. But Matt says Nosey told Blacky they were lovers."

"Salvatore admitted as much to me but blamed Nosey for using him to get a job at the Field Museum."

Stone pointed to the monitor. "There she is again. I guess those women are her new Mahjongg club. Should we ask them about Salvatore?"

"We might need to," Combs said, refocusing on the task at hand.

They watched and tallied Mrs. Slager's visitors for three more hours. Salvatore Bianco never gained access to Mrs. Slager's apartment, according to the tapes. She rebuffed him at least twice a week. One night near the end of the tapes, a blanket or coat was thrown over the camera in the hall. That same night, New Year's Eve, Salvatore wasn't seen leaving the apartment house by the front entrance.

Stone was too quiet. "There's nothing to tie him to her disappearance, is there?"

"Circumstantial. No one will take our fears seriously." Combs wanted to tie up everything for the woman he loved immediately, but investigations were never very efficient processes. "Matt invited me to bunk at his place tonight. I'll see you to the station. You start your new job tomorrow?"

"I'll stay with Mrs. Mack tonight," Stone said. "I'll be all right. I knew in January before Nosey received her hiring offer that my mother wasn't home anymore."

"Should we have a memorial service for her at St. Andrew's?" Combs had read everything he could find about Asperger's online. People were people no matter how their handicaps presented themselves. Stone's emotions filled as wide a scope of feelings as the next person's. Her physical and verbal reactions were more complicated because her mother might not have spent enough time teaching her the fundamentals most children mimic. The poor woman was probably heartbroken after her divorce saddled with an uncuddly baby.

"Let's wait until we find out what really happened. No sense eliciting pity unnecessarily."

"Sympathy for your distress is not pity." Combs touched her dear, sad face.

"I'm glad I have you. Mother worried too much about how I would turn out. She couldn't relax enough to love me."

* * *

Tuesday, May 14
Brighton Condo

Sky had left for work and Grandma was still sleeping upstairs, when Drape opened the door to find Salvatore Bianco getting out of his Lincoln.

He reached her doorstep before she could collect her wits.

His white hair was tousled, but she stepped into his arms for a friendly hug. Proverbs 8:17 comforted her: "For I love them that love me and those that seek me early shall find me."

Drape breathed in the exotic scent she now identified with how all fathers smelled. It was a familiar smell. For a moment she imagined the chemicals which sperm banks used to freeze their male members must contain a similar smell. Could she fill the emptiness in her life, of never being able to identify her father, with this new friend?

"It's a beautiful day," Salvatore said. "Mrs. Mack thought you might have time to show me rental properties in Ann Arbor." His charming smile felt like sunshine on Drape's shoulder. "Professor Carrington says hello. I checked on my latest shipment of crates with him this morning."

Salvatore reached for Drape, but she stepped back into the hall. "You're awfully beautiful this early in the morning. You and Mrs. Mack convinced me Ann Arbor is a better place to live than Chicago."

"Come in, come in," Drape said. "Help yourself to the coffee. It's still hot. I'll leave a note for Grandma that we've gone to find you a new home in Ann Arbor."

A few minutes later, Salvatore opened the passenger door of his black Lincoln for Drape.

Sky let her open her own door, which was all right, but Salvatore's gentlemanly conduct made Drape feel particularly feminine. "I suppose Mrs. Mack had a list all prepared."

Salvatore laughed with his tone of contagious mischief. "Probably receives kickbacks or a percentage of each sale."

"I don't think she has time to pursue a realtor's license." Privately, Drape agreed.

After they'd toured five different apartment properties, Salvatore called a halt. "Which restaurant will it be? You deserve a free lunch for spending so much time with me."

"Hey, what are friends for?" Drape banged Salvatore's shoulder with her backhand.

He stood still, like her touch had transformed him into an inert statue. He ran his hand through his white hair to awake from some deep thought. "Is Charlie's okay?"

"I like the Pizza House better," Drape said. "It's livelier and the menu is bigger."

After a meal of soup and pizza, Drape didn't want to end their time together. "We didn't check out Ike's loft apartments. I wonder if the owner wants to flip them to recover his renovation expenses. Shall I call her? Professor Clarke will understand."

Ike was less than enthusiastic but agreed to meet them at her place.

Salvatore and Drape decided to walk through Gallup Park to give Ike time to get home.

The trees were budding like crazy and the grass held the bright yellow-green glow of springtime. Drape could smell the damp earth rich with promise. "No wonder brides choose this time of year to marry."

She felt like twirling around, letting her childish urges erupt under Salvatore's adoring gaze. The ducks were calling their urgent pleas to each other.

Drape danced around Salvatore, laughing as he tried to catch her in his arms. She ran ahead and then took pity on his lumbering walk. "You've driven a long way today too."

"You understand us old men."

* * *

Ike's Apartment Building

After Ike opened the door to her spacious loft, her frown never eased, even though Salvatore could not have been more agreeable.

"Is Professor Clarke giving you a rough time?" Drape asked. "I thought he would be easy to work for."

"No problem there," Ike said. "Applied Physics is a new program, so I'm able to set up my own filing systems. Rackham has everything online, but Professor Clarke keeps things personal for the small group of students. They're all bright and eager." Still the lines on her forehead deepened. "Are you meeting Sky later?"

"No time for grooms today," Drape said.

Salvatore laughed, but Ike stayed stern.

Drape and even Salvatore made approving comments about Ike's furniture. "Sky said he helped you pick out your furniture. Grandma and I bought more traditional pieces." She remembered Mrs. Henderson's dishes, but Ike was not offering them so much as coffee, so there was no opportunity to mention the gift. "Salvatore's going to buy rental property in Ann Arbor. He loves our town as much as we do."

Salvatore asked, "Could I talk to the owner of your complex?"

Ike was blunt. "Not if Drape wants to keep me as a friend. I just moved in. If Mr. Bianco buys this place, I'll break my lease and move!"

"Don't be ridiculous," Drape said. "What's wrong with you?"

"You," Ike said. "You may have brains enough for four people, but you can't see a snake in the grass at your feet."

Drape pulled Salvatore to the door. "I think you should apologize. Mrs. Mack will hear about your rudeness."

Ike stayed adamant. "Mrs. Mack knows I never doublespeak. I doubt she knows Salvatore's even in town."

"Nonsense!" Drape couldn't figure out Ike's ire. "I'll call you later."

"Is she jealous?" Salvatore asked as they walked back to his car in the warming sun.

"Not a clue," Drape said. She wondered if Ike knew something about Salvatore no one had told her. "She'll call me later to apologize."

Salvatore didn't start the engine immediately. "She's not attracted to me." He sounded surprised and then explained. "When I meet women, I lead with my hips. Other men lead with their heads."

Drape smiled at his prideful attitude. His next subject shocked her. "I read Mother Teresa's diaries, did you?"

Drape indicated she hadn't. "School has been so demanding."

"She complained God wasn't answering her prayers." Salvatore ruffled his beautiful hair. "In fact she felt abandoned."

Drape reached up to pat down a stray lock of Salvatore's hair.

He closed his thumb and forefinger around her wrist, lightly, playfully. "She didn't understand," he said. "God wanted her to go to India to teach birth control, don't you agree?"

Drape didn't pull away. Salvatore was so intent on her answer. "Is that what you think?"

"Yes," he said, releasing his hold. "Did Sky get you pregnant?"

Drape laughed. "Of course not, Salvatore. He knows I'm a Christian and believe marriage is a sacrament."

"I had myself fixed." Salvatore's blue eyes were intense. She thought he might weep. "I don't want to bring innocent children into this horrible world."

Drape thought she understood. He was upset about Ike being so mean to him. "Salvatore, we can't make our friends like each other. I'm very fond of Ike and don't understand her reaction to you. Gee whiz, she's my maid of honor."

"Maybe it's Sky we should ask," Salvatore said.

"Oh," Drape sympathized immediately. "Wouldn't it be sad if Ike were in love with Sky?"

"Very sad," Salvatore said. Drape knew he couldn't have been more sincere.

On the way back to Brighton, Salvatore's light-hearted mood seemed spent. He motioned toward their destination. "Are you sure Sky is the right man for you?"

Drape smiled. "You are kind to worry. I never experienced fatherly concern before. I don't know how to reassure you, but Sky is the best man I know."

"You haven't met many," Salvatore said. Then he added, as if to assuage any seriousness, "Are you sure my interest is only platonic?"

"I certainly hope so," Drape said. "My belief system doesn't allow any straying from the righteous path, does yours?"

He didn't answer and Drape was sure their artless teasing had caused him some embarrassment. When they arrived back at the Brighton condo a little past two o'clock, Salvatore didn't get out of the car. Drape began to open the door, but he reached across her to shut it. "Stay," he said.

"No time left," Drape said. "Is Mrs. Mack cooking you supper?"

"Probably," Salvatore said. "Thank Sky for me."

When Drape opened the condo's front door, Sky had his hand on the doorknob, ready to leave. "Where are you going?" Drape asked.

* * *

"Where have you been with Salvatore?" Sky's question wasn't meant to be friendly. "Did you kiss him?"

Drape's hazel eyes widened. "You're jealous of that old man? I helped him decide which apartment to buy in Ann Arbor. Mrs. Mack sent him. She knows I don't start my calculus class until the fall. Ike and Stone were both working. We visited Ike."

"Neither of them would spend a minute alone with the likes of Salvatore Bianco." Sky didn't feel like being reasonable. "And they're not engaged!"

"Grandma," Drape called. When her grandmother appeared from the kitchen, Drape asked. "Didn't you give Sky my note?"

"Now, Drape," Grandma said. "We both saw Salvatore try to keep you in the car. One of your friends and another friend's mother both had truck with that man, and they're both missing!"

Drape started to cry. "I thought you would understand. He's interested in me, like a father, or a Dutch uncle—you know."

Grandma shook her head. "Don't lie to yourself, Drape. You know your reactions are not those of a daughter."

"I don't!" Drape yelled. "How am I supposed to know? You and Mother decided I didn't need to learn how to trust a father figure." She took off her glasses to see better. "I'm out in the woods here alone!"

Sky believed her. He hoped he could trust her. "I love you, Drape."

"I'm so glad you do." Drape flew at him.

Her cheeks were wet with tears, and he kissed them away. Thankfully, Grandma stayed in the room or their reunion would have progressed.

The telephone rang and Grandma picked it up, saying, "Saved by the bell."

Drape waved the phone away, so Sky answered.

Blacky Schultz sounded excited. "Let me talk to Drape." Sky hit the speaker button before giving the device to Drape. "I found my key when Matt helped me turn the mattress. I told them someone had slept in my bed. I should probably buy a new mattress now. Wait, wait. Let me explain. I'm so upset. Drape, I recognized Nosey's handwriting in the note tied to the key. It's really crazy. Is Combs back with Stone yet?"

"Read it to me," Drape said, shrugging her shoulders at Sky.

"Okay, but before I read it; remember the bed trick in *Measure for Measure*?" Blacky's voice went up another octave. "The note reads, 'Guess who's waiting for you!' Salvatore would recognize my key. It has my apartment number on it. Nosey was complaining about Salvatore's fixation with me. I tried to make light of it, but I think she lured him into my apartment."

"And what?" Drape was getting more and more angry. "Are you accusing Salvatore of sleeping with Nosey? We already know that."

Blacky's voice lost its verve. "I'll call Combs. I think Salvatore was the last person to see Nosey alive. And I don't think he would appreciate being tricked."

"I just spent all afternoon with him," Drape said. "He's buying rental property in order to live in Ann Arbor."

"Where did you find the key?" Sky asked.

"Between the mattress and the box spring," Blacky said. "I guess Nosey stuffed it under when she got frightened. She must have wanted to leave a clue for us. Salvatore's the only one Nosey would have given my key to—to fool him into thinking he was going to bed with me."

"Why don't you come back to Ann Arbor?" Grandma said.

"I like my job," Blacky said. "If Salvatore is in Ann Arbor, I guess I'm safe. If I can't reach Combs, please have him call me."

"We will," Sky said. As he hung up the phone he started to dial Combs' number.

"Don't," Drape said. "Combs will think we're both idiots. Nosey could have left the note as a gag for Blacky. I'll ask Salvatore about it."

"Don't you dare," Grandma said. "Sky, if you don't call Combs, I'll call the police."

* * *

Drape felt like her head was going to burst with all this craziness. They didn't know Salvatore. How could they even imagine the man would harm a friend of hers?

From the speaker phone, she listened to Sky inform Combs of the silly note Nosey had left. Combs said he would call Blacky immediately.

To enhance everyone's state of alarm Combs asked, "Was Matt with Blacky, when she called?"

"Sorry," Sky said, "We didn't hear Matt's voice."

They could hear the added anxiety creep into Combs' voice. "Would you call Mrs. Mack to make sure Stone arrived? I called her cell, but the train may have rocked her to sleep."

Sky assured Combs he would make the call.

"And, Sky," Combs added, "make sure Drape stays away from that creep."

Drape was amazed at the height of paranoia growing unchecked among her friends. They were imagining more terrors than the *Rocky Horror Picture Show*.

Mrs. Slager had probably found a better place to live in Evanston. And Nosey? Nosey could take care of herself if she were tied to the rails before an oncoming freight train. Salvatore was no monster. He was gentle and caring, offering to watch over the girls in Chicago. Okay so he decided to move to Ann Arbor. Salvatore knew she cared for him, when no one else gave a rap. She appreciated his fatherly counsel and support, and he was happier around her.

Everyone else was suffering some sort of relocation anxiety as far as she was concerned. Even Grandma had bought into the business of blaming Salvatore, because Drape had been too honest about her confused physical attraction to him. Good grief, it wasn't like she wanted to dump Sky. Although, marriage might need to be put on a back burner until everyone's simmering jealousies cooled down—especially Ike's.

* * *

Wednesday, May 15
Pastor Nieman's Second Floor Apartment
Main Street, Ann Arbor

Drape immediately fell in love with Pastor Nieman's black-and-white terrier. She sat on the floor, and the puppy jumped into her lap. "What's his name?"

"Mikey," Pastor Nieman said. Sky was frowning. "I'll just put him in the kitchen while we talk. He's hungry."

Mikey whined when Pastor Nieman lifted him away from Drape. "If you ever need someone to watch him ..."

But Sky's scowl deepened. "Pastor, I should say up front, I'm not a believer."

Drape started to defend Sky, but Pastor Nieman held up his hand. "I'm pretty good at my job." He laughed. "Let's go through my routine, and then we'll address your concerns about not sharing a common belief system. You believe in electricity, don't you, Sky?"

Sky waved his hand at the ridiculous question.

Pastor Nieman concentrated on Drape. "How did you meet Sky?"

"My teaching assistant for advanced calculus." Drape pointed at Sky with some pride. "I was so young; I think he thought I might need extra help."

"Which you didn't?"

"Not with math." Drape laughed. "But when I realized he would graduate and I might lose sight of him; I decided Sky was the one. You know, to be the father of my children. Proverbs 9:9 was my reading for that day: 'Give instruction to a wise man and he will be yet wiser; teach a just man, and he will increase in learning.' Sky is so steady. His integrity is noticeable to everyone." Draped watched Sky's face as she added, "Especially Ike."

"How do you have fun together?" Pastor Nieman made a notation on a list on his clipboard.

Sky smiled. "I'm happy spending time with Drape and her friends. Drape is always in a good mood—you know, positive slants on everything. Maybe it's just our age difference, but she has so much energy. She's enthusiastic about everything, especially starting a family."

"We've been busy with graduation and the wedding shower," Drape said. "My grandmother lives with us in Brighton."

"What don't you like about Drape, Sky?" Pastor Nieman clicked his pen.

"Salvatore Bianco," Sky said. "He's a creepy old guy, and she thinks he's some kind of father figure in her life, because her mother used a sperm bank."

Drape sent a prayer skyward. *Lord, I already designed my wedding dress.* Why couldn't people see Salvatore Bianco's good points? Maybe Sky wouldn't marry her.

"And you, Drape? What don't you like about Sky."

"How can Sky presume to believe there is no God? He can't prove there is no God. Even Salvatore believes and he's a scamp."

"See," Sky said pointing at Drape.

Pastor Nieman stood. "We need to meet again, but in the meantime I want both of you to explore your motives for jealousy. Drape, you mentioned another person, Ike? Sky, does love mean you own another person? Love has no bounds, no depths. When we are right with the Lord the living waters of love are bountiful enough for each child in the family you both envision. Your life together will need each and every friend you can court. Marriage is not a reason to isolate together. Marriage is the foundation of our society. You will need to include more and more people in your lives. Do you both understand me?"

Drape held out her hand to Sky, and they embraced before leaving the Pastor's study.

* * *

Brighton Condo

When they got back to the condo, Mother Taylor had joined Grandma. Both jumped to their feet.

"Matt called," Grandma said.

Drape's mother held out her arms for her daughter. "Blacky's gone missing too."

"No," Drape said. Not able to move, she yelled at Sky, "See, Salvatore is with Mrs. Mack!" Maybe something had happened to Mrs. Slager, Nosey, and now Blacky, but Salvatore could not have been involved. Her friends had disappeared and another was being maligned with circumstantial implications. Drape succumbed to her grandmother's consoling arms. She whispered into Grandma's shoulder. "I prayed for their safety."

Why did the Lord need this to happen? Where was His love now? Why had He withdrawn His promise to answer prayers of faith? Drape examined her soul and discovered the excessive joy Salvatore Bianco provided. Drape rocked back and forth in Grandma's arms. *Lord,* she prayed, *forgive me for my sins known and unknown. Help us find the truth. And, Lord, You will not mine be done.*

When they called Mrs. Mack with the bad news and asked about Salvatore, she told them she hadn't seen Salvatore and was stunned to hear he'd been in town. "He never picked up a list of apartment houses the local realtors assembled for him."

For the first time, Drape entertained a doubt about the integrity of Salvatore Bianco. *Lord,* she beseeched, *where there is darkness let me find light.*

She turned to Sky, whose concern for her safety was causing him to snap at her. Now she understood. He wasn't jealous of her affection. He trusted her. She reached for Sky's warm hand. "Sky, Salvatore assured me Mrs. Mack provided him with the names of apartments we visited."

Sky enfolded her in his arms. "We've been trying to warn you."

Between sobs, Drape asked, "But why did he lie to me?"

Mother Taylor answered. "One of the symptoms of psychopathic behavior is lying when there is no reason to."

CHAPTER NINE

Thursday, May 16
Chicago's Field Museum

Larry Combs followed Matt North up three different elevators to the Human Resource offices in the Field Museum, but Combs was the one to show his badge and gain access to the Personnel Director's office. "My assistant," Combs said including Matt in the interview.

"Salvatore Bianco," the gray-headed curator stood behind his desk waving them toward the two chairs facing him. "I knew sooner or later that rapscallion would get into a scrape he couldn't talk himself out of. Charmer, isn't he?"

"He was a guard here?" Matt asked.

"Short time," the director said.

"I understood he skinned specimens for the mammal collection," Combs said.

"Not in my lifetime." The director finally sat down. "I've been personnel manager for forty years. The modern term is human resource manager."

"Nosey Peterson and Holly Schultz," Combs probed, "were hired as laboratory assistants?"

"Yes, yes," the director said. "Great references from the University of Michigan for both the girls. Do you mean to tell me Salvatore Bianco knew them?"

"They rented apartments from him," Matt said, standing as the tension grew.

The director shook his head. "They okay?"

"Missing!" Matt said, sitting back down, hard. "Both missing."

"Better go to the police. Salvatore was fired over a year ago for suspicious behavior. He was found on site during nonscheduled hours. And one of the female students complained he was stalking her."

"Why didn't you warn them?" Matt pounded his fists on the arms of his chair.

"Never knew they were connected," the director said. "Or I certainly would not have recommended they rent an apartment from him. Did you meet him?"

"I did," Matt admitted. "But the girls thought he helped them get their jobs and were grateful he was looking out for them, letting them have first choice of his apartments."

Combs stood. "Thank you for your help, Sir. If you'll excuse us, we need to transfer our inquiries to the police department."

"Good luck." The director came around the desk and shook both their hands formally. It gave the impression they'd attended a funeral rehearsal.

* * *

Ike's Loft Apartment

Sky knew his motives were decent and Ike was close to Drape. She was more logical than Stone, who might be prejudiced against Salvatore anyway because of Mrs. Slager's involvement. Sky knocked on Ike's apartment at five thirty in the evening, wondering how he was going to explain his absence in Brighton to Grandma and Drape. The sky was darkening too early.

"Sky?" Ike brushed her long, black hair over her shoulder. "What are you doing here? Is Drape all right?"

"She's as good as she's going to get." Sky hung his head. "I could use a cup of coffee if you have time to talk."

"This better be good," Ike said, allowing him to enter.

"Is Drape in love with Salvatore?"

"As a father figure?" Ike talked while she hit the coffee maker button, which emitted a thunderous amount of noise during the bean grinding process.

"She does?"

"What exactly is your problem, Sky?" Ike's elbows jutted out as she stood with her fists clenched on her hips.

"I don't want to marry a woman who is turned on by another man." Sky noticed his sentence started out calmly enough but he was nearly shouting the last two words. He sat down and waited until Ike had handed him a cup of coffee.

"You know, Sky," Ike began, "Drape isn't the only woman in the world who wants to start a family but worries her parenting skills will not be up to the task. My stepmother is certifiable, if anyone were to inquire. My father, brother, and I have made the best of it, keeping the family together, mainly because no one else will house the nut-case."

"I didn't know," Sky forgot about his dilemma long enough consider Ike. Such a beauty took your breath away. So Ike was ashamed of her father's wife the way Drape hated the absence of a father in her life.

"Mrs. Mack is the closest I've come to seeing how a woman would care for her children. I'm not sure all that polite maneuvering is the way I want to mother my children, although my stepmother's screaming tantrums are certainly not a viable option."

"I think I just want to vent," Sky said. "I'm so frustrated I want to shake Drape until she comes to her senses. Wouldn't you at least think Drape's faith in her Lord would be shaken when she heard Blacky can't be found?"

"What do you mean?" Ike stood. "Blacky is murdered too!"

"We don't know what happened yet, but Salvatore is spending more time with Drape than I like."

"Why aren't you with her, you idiot?" Ike walked to the front door and flung it open. "Get out!"

Sky walked over to her and wrapped her in his arms. "I'm so sorry, Ike. I thought Mrs. Mack would have told you about Blacky by now." He closed the door and guided Ike back to the living room couch.

Ike broke down, sobbing into Sky's shoulder as he held her. Mortified to cause her any unhappiness, he was lost in her grief. He stroked her thick soft hair as he talked about Drape. "Grandma is staying closer to Drape than before, keeping her in view if not physically holding onto her. Mother Taylor has been on the phone constantly. My epitaph will probably read, 'I stayed by her.' Drape shows more interest in keeping Salvatore in Ann Arbor than appears appropriate for my future wife. But I know her heart. Family means everything to young women. I think the human race is bettered by a woman's need to find the best man to start the next family on earth. I admit I let my jealousy unnerve me enough not to notice the real danger a rapacious male like Salvatore presents. Of course, we all should have been more alarmed when we heard Nosey was intimate with the man who dated Stone's mother. I'm sorry, it's a good thing you're not a Christian or you would think me evil, but I wouldn't mind if Salvatore Bianco was no longer living on the same earth I inhabit."

Ike straightened up and laughed. "Oh, get out, Sky. I can't help you understand Drape. I don't understand myself."

"What do you mean?' Sky knew exactly what Ike meant. He had felt her warmth, knew she hadn't stayed close to him for solace.

"Men!" Ike laughed again. "You idiots don't even know when a girl's in love with you."

Sky stared at her as he headed for the door. "Forgive me," was all he was able to say as he opened the door to the hall to find Drape staring at him.

* * *

"Now you've done it!" Drape screamed at him.

"He certainly hasn't," Ike said pulling Drape into the apartment after slamming the door in Sky's face.

Drape stared at the closed door. Outside the wind was rising, the sky had turned an ugly shade of yellow-green. Ike was talking to her, but a fog had descended on Drape's ears. Heartbreak, this was what they meant. Drape turned and slid her back down the door, awash in a numbing confusion. Today's passage had warned her, Proverbs 9:13: "A foolish woman is clamorous: she is simple and knoweth nothing." Now she knew: there would be no wedding after all.

"I know you love him," she finally said.

"So what?" Ike pulled her to her feet. "He's marrying you."

"I don't want to marry anyone," Drape said. "I should just get a puppy."

"Be too hard on the dog," Ike said. "And what about the heavenly family you were going to add to the world's population?" Ike sat down on the couch.

"Families don't cheat on each other."

"Friends don't either. Sky came to talk about your fidelity. He's worried about Salvatore's influence on his future wife."

"But he came here!" Drape's anger was subsiding, but she didn't want to let her friend off the hook quite yet.

"You know Salvatore isn't welcome here. And Sky knows I think Salvatore is a dangerous faker." Ike went into the kitchen and returned with two cups of coffee. "Drink up before it turns bitter."

Drape did as she was told. "Good coffee." Then she set the unfinished cup on the coffee table in front of her. "You made it for Sky."

"He asked for it," Ike said. "And by the way, families encounter the same vicissitudes friendships endure. There are no guarantees who will love whom. I'm not sure mothers love all their children with the same amount of affection. Surely there are qualifying factors of understanding, loyalties, sympatico personalities. Do you know if you will love all your future children in the same way?"

"I lost Nosey before she went missing," Drape said. "She thought Salvatore was in love with me."

"I wouldn't mind Salvatore loving you. I think Sky loves you the way a husband should. Salvatore's attention wouldn't last a year in a marriage."

"I don't want to marry Salvatore."

"Has he asked you?"

"No, he knows I'm going to marry Sky." Drape wondered if she could be completely honest with Ike. She picked her cup of coffee back up and sipped it. "I know you won't share this with Sky, but Salvatore isn't sure he's the right man for me."

"Sky or himself?"

Drape shook her head. "You know what I mean. Don't be thick. Maybe I'm not cut out for marriage."

"Because your affections are fickle?"

Drape bit her lip. "I admit I'm confused about Salvatore. I'm excited when he's around. Maybe it is not sexually. I like him near."

Ike started braiding small strands of her hair. "I feel excited around Salvatore too. But I'm not confused. I'm afraid of him. He's not really human."

Drape laughed. "Yeah, like in *Moonlight*. He's a wolf!"

"He would bite off his own hand." Ike didn't laugh.

"If he wanted something bad enough," Drape agreed. "I think Salvatore has that much intensity."

"Maybe fear thrills you." Ike finished off one braid with a complicated loop knot and started weaving an identical bunch of hair on the other side of her face, before saying, "I think some women feel too comfortable around a certain breed of men, because there really is no threat to their person, no possibility of sexual intercourse."

Drape laughed. "Hey, you haven't seen Sky smolder when I move in really close. The man is ready and willing. He's just good enough to wait for intimacy until the wedding, because of my faith. I want our marriage to begin the day of our agreement before the Lord, our commitment to stay with each other, forever."

Ike held her unfinished plait still. "I've always thought the reason battered wives remain with their husbands is because they've never known loving intimacy, and they mistake what they are feeling for passion."

Drape got off the couch, took the coffee cups into the kitchen and rinsed them in the sink. Maybe Ike was right about abused women, but she wasn't afraid of Salvatore. "Mother says I've never been frightened of anything."

"You were never scared as a child?"

"No, were you?" Facing the living room windows, she could see trees whipping around and bending too far. "Is there a basement in this place? Turn on the television. We must be under a tornado watch."

Ike was still sitting on her living room couch, hugging a pillow.

Drape turned on the television long enough to hear the siren. She pulled Ike from the couch. "Come on, where's the entrance to the basement?"

"End of the hall," Ike said. "Where's my purse?"

"Forget about it," Drape said picking up her own purse from the floor near the door where she'd dropped it when she was so upset with Sky. "Just grab your keys."

"They're in my purse!"

* * *

No one else was in the laundry room when Drape and Ike arrived. Drape turned on her cell phone, which carried the tornado warning. "I hope Sky gets to a safe place." She bowed her head to pray, remembering Ike was not a believer. *Lord, keep us all safe.*

Ike was still carrying on their previous conversation. "I was scared as a child. One time my stepmother tried to stab Dad. We don't own steak knives now in order to remove the possibility of any future craziness. I was about ten. All four of us were screaming our heads off. I was sure blood would be splattered everywhere, but Dad got the knife away from her. My brother still has nightmares, wets the bed ... and he's fifteen now."

"I have had a peaceful life," Drape said. "The only violence I've seen is on television or in the movies."

"Probably why you don't know what fear feels like. Not having a male in the house is an easy answer, but the violence in my home came from my insane stepmother."

Drape was trying to be completely honest with Ike and herself. "Salvatore treats me as if I'm the most important person in his life. I guess it's natural for Sky to take me for granted."

"You did promise to marry him," Ike said.

Drape nodded her head. "The world doesn't work well if we break our commitments."

"I hear one of Mrs. Mack's dictates." Ike finally laughed.

"I love you, Ike. Please don't be mad at me. Will you still be my maid of honor if I ever decide to marry?"

"You idiot. Of course I will be!" Ike laughed. "What does your phone say now?"

"All clear," Drape said. "Thank you, Lord."

Ike made a tsk noise. "Let's get out of here. You go make up with Sky. Don't let Salvatore sell his lust for love. Sky's the real deal."

"I know you and Sky don't believe in a personal Creator," Drape said. "Did you know Salvatore is a believer?"

"Well, I hope he believes in paying for his crimes in the afterworld." Ike walked Drape to the entrance door. "Weren't you leaving to see Sky?"

Drape didn't step outside, where the sun was shining on the wet pavement. "Should I wait to marry Sky until he's on the same page in terms of religion?"

Ike actually pushed her outside but didn't shut the door. "He was raised not to believe in anything he can't prove."

Drape laughed. "It's not as if he can prove there is no God."

"Goodbye."

"Blessings on your head, true friend."

"Even atheists appreciate blessings from an old and dear friend."
Ike hugged her.

* * *

Chicago Police Station

Matt North's clenched jaw didn't allow him to grind his teeth. He
refused to leave Larry Combs's side.

Compared to Evanston's, Chicago's precinct house held all the
paraphernalia for a Sherlock Holmes-style murder mystery. Bricked-up
windows and an armed guard at the security-scan entrance gate
contrasted with Evanston's sea of glass and hanging philodendrons.

When they inquired at the information desk about Salvatore Bianco's
work history, they were ushered into an interrogation room. With one
uniformed cop stationed at the door, three detectives assembled around
a small metal table.

"How long was he a detective?" Combs asked after his Ann Arbor
detective badge was passed around.

The thick-necked one nodded his head at Matt.

"Matt North. He's a friend of the missing women," Combs said.
"Why this manpower confab when we asked about Bianco's work
record?"

The most tailored and tallest of the three spoke. "Detective Combs,
I'm Nikolai Burress, FBI. We're working in concert with the Special
Victims unit for Chicago. How long have your acquaintances been
missing?"

"Mrs. Slager, mother of a friend of mine, since New Year's Eve. I've
gone through her apartment building surveillance tapes and believe
Salvatore Bianco may have been the last person to see her alive. I gave
Mrs. Slager's computer to the University of Michigan experts to see if
they can find anything to prove he's culpable. We reported her missing
to the Evanston police."

The youngest of the two city detectives stepped out of the room.

"He's going to write up a warrant for a person-of-interest arrest."
Burress seemed to be recreasing the pleat in his slacks. "Why did you
wait until now?"

"I didn't think I had enough evidence, but now two young women
who lived in his apartment house are missing too."

"Idiots," the thick-necked city detective said.

Combs was getting pretty frustrated. "Well, how long did he work here?"

"Never." The young man had reentered. "We know his name from two stalking reports."

Matt stood up. "You let him out on the street—and now ..."

Combs pushed him into his chair. "Give us the forms to fill out."

"Lot of good that will do," the stodgy one said.

Combs shook his head at Matt, who appeared ready to lunge at one of the investigators, unsure of whom to punch first.

Burress seemed to realize their frustration. "Come with us. We have enough evidence to get a search warrant for Bianco's property."

Combs felt it was fitting to share everything at this point. "He owns a wood-working shop in the basement of his apartment building and a dermestids box in the basement of his home."

"Dermestids?" The city cops asked each other.

"Flesh-eating insects." Burress said. "Weren't you a little suspicious?"

"He said he skinned animals for the field museum," Combs said.

Matt had resumed his seat. "We've already talked to the personnel director. Salvatore worked as a guard there for a short time. He was fired because he apparently was in the museum when he wasn't scheduled to work."

"Also," Combs added, "he was found among the collections. I think you're right. I am an idiot. He makes shipping crates for Ann Arbor's Museum. One of the mammal collectors in Ann Arbor told me he'd run across a female leg bone, but I thought he was paranoid because he's sweet on Mrs. Slager's daughter."

"Really," Matt said. "I thought you two ..."

Combs wished he'd kept his mouth shut.

Agent Burress acted as if he refused to judge Combs' personal interest in the case as an impediment. "We need search warrants for two museums, the largest collectors in our region of mammal bones." Burress pinched the perfect pleat in his trousers. "We'll probably need a confession from this freak to get a conviction."

* * *

Nosey Petersen's Top Floor Apartment

Burress instantly dismissed the city detectives, claiming Combs and Matt were motivated to make a thorough search because of their close affiliation with the probable victims. "These two will nail Salvatore Bianco's hide to the wall quicker than a team of forensic experts."

Combs was convinced Matt's need for retribution might compromise any investigation, but there was no conceivable way to keep Matt out of the scene. The odor Drape identified as being Salvatore Bianco's filled Nosey's stuffy top floor apartment.

Matt must have subconsciously sensed the same fact because he went around opening all the windows before upending all the chairs and rolling up the front room's rug. As if exhausted from his frenzy, he finally sat down on Nosey's bed. "I'm trying to let her spirit escape to a more peaceful place."

Combs stared out the bedroom's window, which faced the courtyard's garden. "I remember flowers down there. There's not a bud in sight. Someone has picked every flower."

"Maybe the storm swept them away," Matt said.

Burress hadn't interfered with Matt's illogical actions. "Might as well open all the cupboards and drawers in the place too." He winked at Combs, but Matt proceeded to carry out his orders.

Combs was busy studying Nosey's unusual leather negligees when Matt burst back into the bedroom holding a book aloft.

"Her diary," Matt said. "It was behind a row of books in the living room. Obviously she wanted to hide the evidence from Salvatore Bianco."

CHAPTER TEN

Combs immediately read the last entry in Nosey's diary to Matt and Burress: "Salvatore will appreciate the bed trick from *Measure for Measure* if I have anything to do with it."

Matt was pacing in the front room, not a good sign. "I'll find him," he said. "God willing, I'll find him first."

Burress reached out his hand for the book, but Combs wanted to review a few dates. July 4 read, "I think I've found the one. Salvatore Bianco is the finest specimen of manhood I've seen to date. He could be a Chicago mobster, but who cares. I bet he's a tiger in bed."

July 5 was more alarming, so he didn't read it out loud. *Stone's mother showed up at Salvatore's. I was still in his bed. She yelled at me! Salvatore had gone to buy coffee. Mrs. Slager says I'm taking my life in my hands. What a load! She is one angry, jealous woman. She says she's going to move out of Salvatore's apartment just to keep Stone safe. Salvatore doesn't give a rap for our catatonic sorority sister. He thinks she's retarded, which of course she isn't. I guess his ego is big enough he thinks any woman who doesn't find him appealing has to be stupid. I think Stone is so innocent, she doesn't even realize her mother is having an affair with Bianco.*

Burress asked to read the diary after Combs read the rest of the entries to himself. Combs realized Matt had already surmised the machinations of Nosey's suicidal conspiracy.

"Nosey got Blacky killed." Matt's head was down but not in resignation. He appeared to be pawing the ground about to charge into something.

"I need to get back to Stone," Combs said, hoping Matt would understand his need to keep one woman safe.

"Keep Drape as close to Sky as possible," Matt said. "I may not find Salvatore in time."

Burress didn't take notice of Matt's vigilante threat. "I'm coming with you to Ann Arbor, Combs." He patted Matt on the back. "You stay in Chicago until you hear from us."

* * *

On the private jet Burress flew out of O'Hare airport, Combs read his notes about the case, "July fourth, Bianco in Chicago with Mrs. Slager, Nosey Peterson, and Stone Slager."

Burress asked, "How did you come up with that date?"

"Stone told me, and Nosey lists their visit in her diary. Didn't you read the July fifth entry, where Mrs. Slager confronts Nosey in Bianco's bed?"

"I did," Burress said. "But no one got hurt."

"Not yet," Combs said, continuing to read his notes aloud. "'July fifteenth, Mrs. Slager moves to Evanston. Bianco visits, continually rejected.' Her daughter, Stone, and I reviewed the two cameras in Mrs. Slager's new apartment. One was of the front entrance and one was in her hallway."

"Circumstantial," Burress said.

"Stone went to Evanston for Christmas, but her mother didn't mention being harassed by Bianco."

"Probably didn't want to alarm her daughter."

"She should have," Combs said. "Stone recommended Bianco as a body guard for her sorority sisters, Nosey Peterson and Blacky Schultz, the two girls who are missing."

"When did you report Mrs. Slager as missing?"

"Not until Stone and I reviewed the tapes on May thirteenth. On New Year's Eve, Mrs. Slager's hall camera was covered, and we didn't see Bianco leave from the front entrance."

"Same level of evidence, circumstantial."

"I know, I know." Combs searched his notes. "Stone spoke to Bianco when he was still in Chicago on January thirteenth, which was when Stone made a conference call from her sorority to introduce Bianco to the girls. She'd left messages for her mother, but of course they weren't answered. On January nineteenth Bianco showed up in Brighton with Mrs. Mack to be introduced to the girls. He stayed in his fraternity next to Sigma Kappa in Ann Arbor until March twenty-second, when he took the girls to a Shakespeare play at the Goodman Theatre. I went along to search for Mrs. Slager."

"Is that when you took the computer back to the university?" Burress asked. "By that time Mrs. Slager had been missing for three months and Bianco had traveled—probably several times—back and forth between Chicago and Ann Arbor."

Combs was thankful the man's memory was right on target. "On May eleventh I met a paleontology professor at a wedding shower at the sorority. They'd found a female leg bone in their collection. Professor Carrington told me about it because he's romantically involved with Stone Slager, or wishes he were. Bianco was there, but he didn't hear what the professor had to say. Matt and the missing Blacky attended the shower too. They said Bianco was supposed to bring Nosey Peterson. That's what she had told them in Chicago on the ninth of May."

"They didn't see her on the tenth? How many young women are in the sorority? Are any of them in imminent danger?"

Combs looked out the airplane's window as they crossed Lake Michigan. At first he thought a sailing regatta was underway, but on closer inspection he saw white caps had fooled him. "The four of them are very close. Drape Taylor wanted a bodyguard for them, so Stone suggested Bianco. Ike St. Claire has her own apartment in Ann Arbor now, as does Stone. Drape is living with her grandmother and fiancé in Brighton. All four girls worked in the Zoology Museum. Drape has a PhD in statistics and will be teaching calculus in the fall. Stone and Ike both have jobs as administrators at the university too."

* * *

Brighton Condo

Drape had hoped Sky's van would still be parked outside Ike's apartment building, but he'd gone home in disgrace. As she drove her Ford up Route 23, she could see the storm clouds moving ahead of her. She prayed the twenty-third Psalm: *The Lord is my shepherd, I shall not want.* But she did want. She wanted Sky and Salvatore to be friends, like family. Dreaming of course. She was daydreaming. She would need to choose, eventually. Not today. What would Sky tell Grandma? That she'd caught him at Ike's?

He maketh me to lie down in green pastures; He leadeth beside the still waters. The grass was surely greening along the road, but there were no still waters in her soul. A whirlpool of descending thoughts taunted her. Mrs. Slager murdered or living elsewhere? Nosey so embarrassed by Salvatore's rejection, she'd left her apartment? And Blacky, why would Blacky not be in touch with Matt? Salvatore didn't have the answers any more than she did. Was she the only human on earth who saw Salvatore Bianco's good qualities? He was no villain. He couldn't be in her life, if the Lord didn't want him there.

He restoreth my soul. Drape didn't understand the hatred around her for a man she admired, one who understood her need for a father. Of course, misunderstandings happen the way Ike described, but every single person she knew mistrusted Salvatore. Was she wrong? Anyway she could forgive them. When Salvatore was vindicated, they would need her understanding.

He leadeth me in paths of righteousness for His name's sake. Yeh, though I travel through the valley of the shadow of death, I shall fear no evil. Somehow the day at the sorority came to mind, when she felt a chill but no one had entered the hall. Could that have been Mrs. Slager's ghost, trying to warn them?

For Thou art with me, Thy rod and Thy staff they comfort me. Drape pitied Ike and Sky for not being able or willing to tap her source of strength. No wonder they were drawn to each other—by what, a lack of solace?. These were not pleasant thoughts. They were fearful, and fear does not proceed from the Lord.

Thou preparest a table before me in the presence of mine enemies … Were Mother, Grandma and Sky planning to give her a going-over when she got home? Were her family members now Salvatore's enemies? *Thou annointeth my head with oil. My cup runneth over. Surely goodness and mercy will follow me all the days of my life, and I will dwell in the house of the Lord, forever and ever.*

The Ford turned into the condo's driveway, but Drape was loath to get out of the car.

* * *

Sky tapped on Drape's window. Her hazel eyes were wet with tears. She pushed the button for the window to descend.

"Did Ike explain?" he asked.

"She loves you, but she is my maid of honor." Drape opened the car door. "What did you tell Grandma and Mother?"

"Isn't this bad enough without encouraging their bad opinions of me?" Sky dropped his arms to his sides.

Drape gave him a small smile. "They'd be on your side."

"Did you go to the basement during the storm? Traffic was terrible in town. I parked under the railroad bridge on Washington until it was over." He held out his arm, and she stepped close to his side. "I love you, you dope," he said. "I'm worried Salvatore will take you away from me." Sky pushed away and doubled over in real pain. He gasped, "Everyone he knows is disappearing."

"Don't, Sky." Drape pulled at his shoulders. "Grandma and Mother will worry if they see you're upset."

"Promise me you won't see him alone anymore." Sky whisked away a wetness near his eyes.

"I promise, if you promise not to malign him anymore."

Sky knew his side of the promise would be as difficult to keep as hers. "I promise."

Grandma opened the door. "What are you two conspiring about?"

Sky and Drape laughed at not being caught out.

* * *

Friday, May 17
Brighton Condo

Sky opened the door for Combs, who apologized for arriving at the dinner hour. A strong smell of honey-baked ham clued him into the hour. "Let me introduce Nikolai Burress, FBI," Combs said.

Drape hung back, but Mother Taylor quickly arranged two more settings for the table. "Come in, come in."

Grandma issued a blessing for the food they were about to receive.

Drape busied herself with making sure everyone was served the side dishes of sweetened yams, asparagus and cornbread. Since Drape was reticent, Sky started the inquiry, "Have you found the girls?"

"Not yet," Combs said, more interested in his plate's portion of the ham.

Burress set aside polite, phatic comments about the food to converse about the purpose of their visit, "Miss Taylor, I understand one of your professors found a human leg bone?"

Drape reached for her water glass to avoid answering the FBI agent's question; then she shook her head at Sky.

"We'd like you to set up a meeting with the professor." Burress spoke directly to Sky. "I want to gather DNA evidence to see if one of the missing women can be identified."

Mother Taylor gathered the emptied plates into the kitchen. When she returned with a tray of strawberries and pound cake, she asked, "Why is the FBI involved?"

Sky released a burst of laughter. "Sorry, Drape."

Grandma patted Drape's knee. "Seems you involve the government if you ship criminal remains across state lines."

* * *

Sigma Kappa Sorority House

Matt had stayed in Chicago hunting down leads on Salvatore's whereabouts. Combs introduced the very tall FBI agent to Mrs. Mack.

Nikolai Burress shook their hands. Mrs. Mack was dutifully nervous. Stone hardly noticed the man, she was so involved with Combs. But Ike, Ike on the other hand acted as if a new moon had settled too close to the ground for her to remain unmoved.

Drape cocked her head at Sky for him to take notice of the seismic shift in the sorority's universe.

Ike relocated herself to the couch facing the fireplace, inviting Burress to sit next to her. He wasn't devoid of senses and rightly evaluated her interest in more than his topic of conversation.

Still in the hall, Combs spoke quietly, but they could all hear him. "We'll need a hair sample from you, Stone, to see if it matches the DNA in Professor Carrington's find."

After providing the hair sample for Burress' evidence bag, Stone joined them in the living room, ending a slight lull in the conversation. "Who knew Salvatore's fixation with museum bones would compel him to add to the collections?"

Mrs. Mack drew in a deep breath, too shocked to comment on Stone's tasteless comment.

Ike laughed. "I'm going crazy. Stone how can you be so removed from a dreadful crime your mother might have been a victim of?"

Drape's voice was too soft, "You all have hung him and Salvatore hasn't even been accused of a crime."

"What?" Sky asked, "I didn't hear you and I'm sitting right next to you."

"No one has proof Salvatore did anything," Drape said. "He says youth is wasted on the young. He says how flagrant young girls are. Is it a crime that he wants to reach out for more of what gives him pleasure, even if it's being with women?"

Grandma used her outside voice: "If Salvatore Bianco is involved with these missing women, the truth will out."

"Actually, Drape," Burress said, "the best way to clear Salvatore would be for you to wear a wire. I suspect he's been stalking you and will contact you at his earliest opportunity. He'll ask to meet you alone."

Drape's head felt like it would explode with conflicting emotions. Proverbs 10:3 provided a modicum of inner strength: "The Lord shall not suffer the soul of the righteous to famish; but he casteth away the substance of the wicked."

So Sky asked her, "Why don't you wait until you talk to Professor Carrington?"

Drape used the speakerphone when she called the professor. They were all taken aback by his questions about Stone's wellbeing. "Yes, she is here," Drape said. "Detective Combs will be joining us too."

* * *

University of Michigan, Zoology Museum

The entire lynching gang assembled outside Carrington's office: Mother Taylor, Grandma, Burress, Ike, Combs Burress, and Stone. Drape seemed to be shrinking as the proof piled up against Salvatore Bianco. Sky had to admit the girl was loyal in the face of overwhelming odds. Loyalty was not a bad trait for a wife, was it?

If Salvatore were found culpable, would Drape turn to Sky as a consolation prize? Removing Salvatore might not solve the real problem. Was Drape in love enough to even attend their wedding in June? Sky wanted to be first in her life, not second best. Maybe eighteen was too young to marry.

After this Salvatore-problem got sorted out, they could reconsider their relationship. Sky thought he should move back in with his folks, give Drape some space and time to evaluate the upcoming marriage contract. His heart started thudding in his chest. He couldn't lose her. She was such a beauty, so bright, and everyone loved her. Who wouldn't? He felt separated already from her gracious form, removed from her awareness.

Sky pushed to move closer, between Grandma and Mother Taylor, but neither would give an inch. He touched Drape's back, and she jumped as if a stranger had touched her.

"Oh, Sky," she said. "I didn't know you were behind me."

Sky had let go of her shoulder. He wondered if he would ever feel her touch again.

Carrington opened the door and all eight of them filed into the space remaining between file cabinets, tables, and a desk surrounded with boxes of published papers. After Drape introduced them all, Burress asked to see the specimen in question.

Carrington had stored the leg bone in his office, behind his coat rack. "Didn't know where to keep it safe."

"Professor," Drape asked, "you don't believe Salvatore Bianco could have smuggled this in here, do you?" After a pause, Drape said, "You liked him."

"Charming man, but Salvatore's the one who pointed out how lax our security system is." Carrington laid the leg bone on his paper-cluttered desk. "If anyone could figure out how to dispose of bones, it would be Salvatore Bianco."

Drape's grandmother moved to shield Stone from seeing the bone, which might be her mother's, but Combs had already ushered her back into the hallway.

Burress had brought his evidence box. He donned his sterile gloves and quickly chipped off a small piece of the gristle near what was the knee end of the bone. After bagging the evidence and labeling it, he turned to them. "I'll take this down to the federal forensics lab in Milan in the morning to rush it through with Stone's hair sample."

Drape sighed. "Okay, wire me up Coach. If Salvatore's own words won't clear him, I guess I'll have to agree with the rest of you."

Sky didn't feel the elation he'd expected. Was his future bride already his ex-girlfriend? She was keeping her distance already.

* * *

Saturday, May 18
Brighton Condo

"Am I the only one who thinks Salvatore Bianco could be innocent?" Drape asked Grandma as they loaded the breakfast dishes into the dishwasher.

"I'm afraid so, dear." Grandma slapped her bottom. "Burress and Combs say they will follow you and Salvatore." Grandma quickly sat down on one of the chairs. "Please be careful. I wish I had enough money to protect you, but this is something you must do for your own peace of mind."

"I'm not a bit afraid." Drape hugged her. "Please don't worry. Sky took off work to stay with Combs. Did Sky tell you why he moved back with his folks? I know Salvatore would never hurt me."

"Sky is taking your fixation with Salvatore to heart," Grandma said as Drape helped her on with her coat. "Your mother and I will want to know as soon as you're safe."

"You'll be the first people I call," Drape promised. "Sky needs time to sort out his jealousy about my wanting a father before I want a husband."

"You don't have a father," Grandma said, "And Salvatore Bianco's interest in you is not fatherly. You know that in your heart."

"I don't know anything of the kind." Drape wanted to rant about her mother's decision to use a sperm bank; but the old excuse no longer fit the circumstances. "What's wrong with having an older friend?"

Grandma shook her head. "You know what's right, Drape. Salvatore doesn't want you to marry Sky, does he?"

"He's not sure Sky is the right man for me, just like any father would worry about his daughter."

"No, Drape. You'll find out Salvatore has other intentions. At least we'll all be listening to what he has to say."

Drape compared her grandmother's warnings to her morning's reading in Proverbs 10:8: "The wise in heart shall receive commandments, but a prating fool shall fall."

Burress was right about one thing, Salvatore must have been keeping watch on the condo, because he knocked on the door not ten minutes after Grandma drove away.

"He's here," Drape said into the wire before she took her time opening the door. "Salvatore, thought you would be in Chicago, finding a buyer for your mother's house."

"No such luck, so far." Salvatore held out his arms. "Where's my hug?"

Drape dutifully hugged him, as she thought a daughter would. He was innocent, wasn't he? She imagined Sky was not happy picturing this latest development from wherever they were listening.

"Coffee?" Salvatore asked.

"Still some in the pot." Drape hoped he wouldn't want to go to a restaurant. She felt safer in the condo.

"Won't Sky worry if the neighbors tell him I was here?"

"Don't be silly. Sky understands how I feel about you."

"Really?" Salvatore's voice dropped its friendly tone. "How do you feel about me?"

"You're my friend," Drape said honestly; then she hedged her bet. "You know, like a Dutch uncle?"

"Platonic?" Salvatore opened the front door. "No harm in taking a ride with a friend?"

Drape finished pouring two cups of coffee, ignoring his invitation. "Grandma will be back soon to take me shopping." She noticed one of the cups rattled a bit as she set it down. "Did you see all the dishes we got at the shower?"

Salvatore closed the door and came over to the table without sitting down. "I thought bridal showers were for lingerie?"

"Not when men are invited. Blacky ..." Drape coughed. "Blacky wanted Matt's father to be invited."

Salvatore pulled her to him by her waist. "Orlando, wasn't that his name?"

Drape laughed, she hoped nervously enough for whoever was listening to head her way. Salvatore was too suspicious to tell her anything. "Blacky is missing!" She maneuvered to a chair next to him at the table. "Oh, do you want a bagel with your coffee?"

"No. The coffee is good. Who said Blacky was missing?"

"Matt called," she said.

"That boy is always missing something." Salvatore laughed before joining her at the table. "Nosey told me Ike dumped him and Blacky picked him up out of pity."

"Something like that." Drape concentrated on her emptying cup.

"Do you want to listen to a cautionary tale?" he asked.

Drape cocked her head to encourage him. "Remember when you said Mrs. Mack gave you a list of houses?" Drape's swallowing was suddenly difficult. Did she indeed trust this man? Then, why were her hands beginning to sweat? The coffee cup was cold.

"No." Salvatore traced a circle on the tablecloth. "You asked me if she had and then we talked about her kickbacks."

"That's right," Drape admitted. "What did you want to tell me?"

"I want a woman I love to love me."

"That's everyone's wish," Drape felt comfortable enough to smile and pat Salvatore's hand.

He grabbed her hand with too much force, and her cup spilled its dregs on the tablecloth.

"Oh, here, let me clean this up." Drape scurried into the kitchen. She wanted to yell, "Help! Help, you idiots! Knock down the door!" But instead she ran water onto a dishtowel and slowly walked back to the table to mop up the coffee.

Salvatore watched her silently, took a deep breath and said, "I want you to move away with me, away from my past crimes which are about to be revealed."

"Why Salvatore, what crimes?" Drape asked, emboldened by his honesty.

"Nosey and I were fooling around in my house." Salvatore waited for Drape to comment.

"When was this?" Drape's brain was a lot calmer than the rest of her.

Salvatore cocked his head, as if evaluating her reason for asking. "The night before your wedding shower. What day was that?"

Drape swayed back and forth in her chair, trying to remember the elusive date. "The day before? May eleventh was my shower. You were there. Remember Sky made a joke about never going to bed angry?"

Salvatore didn't flinch. "He thought that old dame said, 'Never go to bed.'"

Drape remembered their audience. "Rose Grace Warner is a very elegant woman."

"Sorry," Salvatore tipped his head. "You'll be more beautiful at her age."

"Thanks," Drape said, not able to control the conversation as much as she would have liked.

Salvatore tapped the table to get her undivided attention. "So on May tenth, Nosey Peterson was running around my house in Chicago naked, daring me to make love to her. She ran down into the basement and sashayed over to the dermestids box. Then she started kidding about how small Mrs. Slager was."

"'You could shove Stone's mom in this box and be rid of her.'" Salvatore did a nearly perfect imitation of Nosey's voice.

Then, Salvatore finished his coffee.

"What did you say to the crazy girl?" Drape asked aware of the tingling up her back bone.

"I dared her to get in the box." Salvatore's face showed no expression.

Drape wanted to touch the microphone between her breasts but tugged on her ear instead.

Salvatore pulled her head down and looked behind her ear. "Do you have a mosquito biting you?"

"Too much dandruff shampoo." Drape was staggered at her ability to lie so easily.

Salvatore nodded. "So anyway, Nosey got in the box, and I closed the lid, hooting as loud as she was. Then she screamed, and I was laughing so hard, I couldn't breathe. I got hysterical, I guess, and couldn't stop cackling to let her out before it was too late."

"Oh, Salvatore," was all Drape could say, before pandemonium broke out.

The front door burst open.

Sky tackled Drape to the ground and pushed her head down as he scooted her under the table.

When Burress and Combs both jumped on Salvatore's chair, they all three crashed to the floor.

Drape peeked under Sky's protective arm, to see Salvatore escape by wiggling out of his loafers as the three wrestled with each other.

Burress fled after him, running out the front door.

Drape heard a car door slam, squealing tires, and gunfire. For a second, she hoped Salvatore had been killed, to put him out of his misery.

Instead, Burress rejoined them. Combs was sitting on the living room floor, holding both of Salvatore's reeking shoes.

Towering over the three of them on the floor, Burress admitted, "Salvatore escaped."

Thank the Lord, Drape thought. But out loud she confessed her error to Sky. "I was wrong."

Sky still held her in his arms. His face was wet, and he was shaking. "I never should have left you alone with a murderer. I understand why you don't want me for a husband. I don't have enough sense to protect a rabbit."

"Who told you I don't want you for my husband?" Drape asked as she wiped his face with the dishtowel, which had landed on the floor with them. "We're going to marry in June. You are the only man I ever want to touch me, just you."

Sky didn't seem able to let her go, so they sat on the floor until Grandma and Mother arrived about ten minutes later.

Combs presented Salvatore's shoes for observation, while Burress explained what had happened.

Grandma set the world straight. "Now, Sky bring your suitcase upstairs. We need your help arranging all those dishes in the china cabinet."

Burress and Combs said their goodbyes.

Sky finally let go of Drape to get up and kiss Grandma. "Thank you," he said. "Drape is all the home I'll ever need."

* * *

Sunday, May 19
Salvatore Bianco's Home

On the oversized porch, Larry Combs stood behind Nikolai Burress as the FBI agent issued a loud warning before compromising the lock. Matt rushed into the kitchen. They heard him run down the basement steps. Burress stayed in the living room until Matt returned.

"The dermestids box is empty," Matt said and collapsed into a recliner. "But where is that stench coming from?"

"Stay with him," Burress directed. He proceeded up to the second floor. They could hear his footsteps overhead.

"Do you need a drink of water?" Combs asked Matt. He recognized the smell.

Matt shook his head concentrating on the movement upstairs.

Finally, Burress called them. "Combs, best bring that young man up here to identify his girlfriend."

Matt needed Combs' support as well as the handrails. "She's gone," he said. "Now I'll have to kill Bianco."

Combs wanted to permanently divest the lad of any vigilante tendencies, but when they walked into Salvatore's bedroom, he had nothing cautionary to say.

Blacky Schultz was fully clothed, propped up into almost a sitting position, with her lovely red hair combed over her shoulders. Bianco had arranged yellow daffodils and purple violets around her body as if for a funeral viewing.

Blacky's eyes were open and her head slightly cocked. Her position gave the impression that at any moment she might shake herself and talk to them. Bianco had also woven a halo of white crocus for her hair.

Combs understood. "I wondered where all the courtyard flowers from Salvatore's apartment house had gone."

Matt went to pieces. He crumpled to the floor in agony.

Burress closed Blacky's eyes and drew a comforter up over her head. He walked to the window opening it to relieve the smell of death before dialing his phone to summon a forensic team to the address.

Combs spoke as softly as he could, but Matt heard. "Have them check to see if she's been violated."

"How did he kill her?" Matt got to his knees, pulled himself up next to the dresser.

Burress tipped Blacky's head forward. Combs saw the reddened pillow, but Matt was spared the ghastly sight. "Blow to the back of her head."

"She couldn't have felt anything." Combs knew Matt's vengeance was not appeased by the useless information. "Why do you think Salvatore failed to dispatch Blacky's remains the way we suspect Nosey and Mrs. Slager were treated?"

"She was a beauty," Burress said. "I'm not aware of your other friends' appearances."

Combs speculated. "I don't think he was angry with Blacky. Apparently Nosey ruined his relationship with Mrs. Slager."

Burress flipped through his cell phone notes on the case. "When did you notice the flowers were taken from Salvatore's courtyard?"

Matt was still leaning on the dresser. Combs had given him his own handkerchief to cover his nose.

"When we found Nosey's diary." Combs reviewed his notes. "Thursday, May sixteenth."

CHAPTER ELEVEN

Tuesday, May 20
St. Andrew's Episcopal Church

Drape's mother and grandmother sat on each side of her. Thankful there was no necessity to view Blacky's body, Drape concentrated on the enlarged poster Mrs. Mack provided. Blacky Schultz's long red hair was curled in loose ringlets. In the picture, she wore the bridesmaid dress chosen for Drape's wedding. Its emerald-green color brought out the green of Blacky's lovely eyes. And her smile, probably directed at Matt, testified to her warmth and intelligence. All lost. White roses decorated the altar and circled the casket.

Grandma patted Drape's knee, as Drape stopped a sob. Mr. and Mrs. Schultz were sitting in the pew closest to the communion rail. Matt North couldn't be found, but his father, Orlando, attended and offered his condolences to Blacky's parents before sitting down across the aisle from them.

Mother reached for Drape's hand. "Nothing can be said to alleviate their loss."

Drape nodded. *Why, Lord?* She remembered His answer to Job about not being present when the earth was created and therefore unable to understand the machinations of life. And Drape did not understand. Nevertheless, her love for the Lord had not diminished. Proverbs 11:12: "He that is void of wisdom despiseth his neighbor: but a woman of understanding holdeth her peace."

Drape could testify in a court of law that the Lord was with them now, enclosing them in His arms, weeping with them at the loss of one of His most beautiful creatures on earth. And Blacky's soul was present too, loving her parents and waiting with the rest of them for Matt North to show up.

On the way into church, Sky had even asked Drape if her faith in the afterlife was shaken. "I know you prayed continually for their safety as soon as you heard Nosey and Blacky were moving to Chicago."

Drape didn't know how to explain to a nonbeliever. The result of her prayers didn't negate the fact she'd wanted them to be safe. "If I couldn't rely on the Lord listening to me now, when I need Him even more, I don't think I could survive this horror."

Sky had shaken his head, not able to relate to her way of thinking. He sat in the row behind her with Stone and Combs. Combs was dressed appropriately, but Stone had worn a red blouse.

Mrs. Mack, Ike, Ike's brother, their parents, and the FBI agent were seated across the aisle.

After Pastor Nieman said a few comforting words, everyone turned to watch Matt North walk down the aisle, place a white rose on the coffin, and then head for the podium.

Pastor Nieman yielded the post.

"Mr. and Mrs. Schultz," Matt began. "I loved your daughter. She said she loved me too. I don't know when she would have married me, but Blacky said she needed time to prove herself. And now she's gone." He stopped speaking, hung his head, and seemed to forget his audience. Finally, he continued, "Sorry if I offend you, Pastor, or the rest of those who loved my Blacky. But I want you to know, I will not end my days on this earth until I feel retribution has been paid for our loss." With those last angry words ringing throughout the church, Matt walked back out of the building.

His father rose and followed him, waving half-heartedly at Mrs. Mack.

Ike stood, and everyone followed her outside, where the hearse waited to take Blacky's remains to the train station and then back to Florida.

Mr. and Mrs. Schultz requested that no one need attend the burial. "We'll say our goodbyes here," Mr. Schultz said.

"Pray for Matt," Mrs. Schultz said. "We want no harm to come to him."

Ike gently pushed Drape's mother aside in order to take Drape's hand. "We need to help Stone through this," she said.

"And you two," Grandma said.

Stone Slager and Combs approached them. Stone said, "I have good news, to cheer everyone up."

"Now may not be the time," Larry Combs said.

Mrs. Mack stepped closer. "What it is Stone?" She smiled at Combs. "I could use some cheering up."

"Carrington's leg bone was my mother's," Stone said in a triumphant tone.

Pastor Nieman shook his head. "Should we arrange a memorial service for Mrs. Slager?"

"Nobody knew her," Stone said. "We'll never find the rest of her among the collection of bones." She smiled at Combs. "But I want to tell you all something else. Combs has asked me to marry him. Soon. I hope you don't mind, Drape, but we're going to marry here, if you'll have us, Pastor, on Saturday, June first."

Mrs. Mack shook her head and then reached for Combs' hand. "Congratulations. I know our Stone will make you happy."

Drape's mind was slow in shifting from the great loss in her life to understanding how Stone could move on so quickly. "We'll need to find you a dress."

"I'll wear my bridesmaid dress, if you think it's okay." Stone wove her arm around Combs' waist. "I hope you like yellow."

Ike dropped Drape's hand. "You are always full of surprises, Stone." She held out her hand to Combs, but Stone took it and then reached for Drape's hand too.

"Will you two be my bridesmaids?" Stone laughed, and the church echoed the new merriment. "I don't know who to choose for maid of honor. Mrs. Mack, will you be my matron of honor?"

"Of course, Stone," Mrs. Mack dissolved into tears and had to sit down.

Ike's stepmother, a short black-haired Asian woman, sat down next to Mrs. Mack, offering her a fresh handkerchief. The woman shook her head. "Inappropriate," she repeated again and again, trying to receive affirmation from those around her.

Nikolai Burress moved Ike toward his black rental car.

Drape followed them. "Ike," she called. "What should we do?"

Ike had opened the passenger door. "Show up," she said. "I feel like I'm on a merry-go-round. Since January, we've lost two friends, now two more are marrying." She stopped talking and looked across the car at Burress, who still stood next to the driver's door. "And here is this man who, I have to admit, further shakes my timbers."

"Ike," Drape hugged her. "I'm so glad."

"I know," Ike said. "I guess we should just keep moving—like Stone." She smiled at Burress, who got into the rental. But Ike wasn't ready to leave. "Sorry, my stepmother is making such a scene."

"We understand, your mother ..." Drape said.

"I don't," Ike said. "She's not my mother or my brother's mother. I tell everyone Dad married her after mother left him. I never have understood. I suppose it's not really my business anymore."

Drape let her go. "I'll see you June first, if not before."

"Kiss Sky for me," Ike said with a wink.

Drape turned to find Sky at her shoulder. "Ike told me how democratic Salvatore was with his attentions."

"Oh, not now," Drape said. "Please, I need time ..."

"To what?" Sky asked. His eyes snapped in anger. "I'll be staying with my folks for a while. Call me when you've had enough time."

Drape felt like fainting. Grandma steadied her arm. "Come along, dear. Your mother is waiting."

"Sky's going to live with his folks again." Drape couldn't believe the shifting emotional universe of the last few hours. "What will I do?"

"Marry him on the fifteenth as you planned." Grandma marched her to her mother's rental. "Right now, we all need food."

Pastor Nieman called to Drape. "May I have a word?"

"Please join us for lunch," Grandma said. "Do you have time?"

"As a matter of fact, I do," Pastor Nieman said.

Mother took control, opening the passenger's door. "Jump in. We're planning to check out the Gandy Dancer Restaurant. My mother has reserved it for Drape's wedding reception."

* * *

Gandy Dancer Restaurant

The wait-staff scurried about to find Pastor Nieman's group immediate seating. "Sorry for the delay," The young hostess said as she smoothed a wrinkle from the tablecloth. "The flowers along the tracks have just begun to bloom."

Outside on the hillside created by the vehicle bridge over the railroad tracks, flowering redbud trees surrounded by multicolored tulips claimed spring had won the battle against winter's darkness.

"Beautiful," Drape said, dredging a smile from some unknown depths.

Grandma unfolded her napkin before saying, "Combs told me the courtyard was completely stripped of flowers to decorate Blacky's body."

Pastor Nieman's eyebrows pointed south, ruining his usually peaceful and handsome face. "I thought the white roses appropriate for such a young girl."

"Salvatore Bianco apparently decorated Blacky's body." Mother waved for the waiter to take their orders. "Pastor needs to return to church, isn't that right?"

Pastor Nieman smiled, not willing to tell even a white lie. "Why would Mr. and Mrs. Schultz allow Salvatore Bianco to decorate her remains?"

"They didn't," all three women explained.

Mother clarified Grandma's statement. "When Blacky's body was found in Salvatore Bianco's house, it was surrounded with flowers, apparently taken from his apartment house garden."

When the waitress arrived, Pastor Nieman ordered a pork tenderloin, Mother asked for white fish, and Grandma chose a shrimp salad.

"I'm not very hungry," Drape said.

"We've just returned from her friend's funeral," Grandma explained to the waitress.

"I'll give you a moment." The young girl nearly dashed from the table.

"Sky moved out of our condo," Drape explained and then realized she might be further misunderstood. "Grandma was staying with us too."

"Would you like to schedule another session with Sky?" Pastor Nieman asked.

"Yes!" Grandma and Mother answered for her.

Drape nodded. Sky needed to explain his actions and, she needed to come to terms with the facts. Salvatore Bianco had probably killed two of her sorority sisters and the mother of another. "All the time I was praying for Blacky and Nosey's safety, I should have included myself."

"Yes," Grandma said. "We were wrong to let you go to college on your own at sixteen. We weren't in our right minds at the time."

"Speak for yourself," Mother said. "The child has a PhD at twenty years of age and is marrying a professor with tenure-track possibilities. Maybe I should have left home earlier."

* * *

Saturday, May 25
Brighton Condo

Mrs. Mack called at eight o'clock at night, too late to call Sky at his parent's house. "Matt's been arrested."

Drape's first thought was Salvatore had been injured. "Is he all right?"

"Arson," Mrs. Mack said. "He burnt down Salvatore's home and apartment building."

"Will Larry Combs bail him out?" Drape asked.

"Combs and Burress are flying back tonight," Mrs. Mack said. "Drape, Ike tells me you and Sky are not going to be married."

"Yes, we are!" Drape said. "Mother is staying with me to get ready, so Sky is staying with his parents until after the wedding."

"That makes sense," Mrs. Mack said. "I'll call Ike and Stone."

"Stone doesn't think I'm getting married either?" Drape started to wonder if maybe Sky was talking about their separation.

"Ike gossiped with her. Stone was sure you two would marry." Mrs. Mack coughed. "Stone is an unusual friend, but loyal."

"I agree," Drape said. "Let me know if you hear more about Matt. He's going to be Sky's best man."

"Oh, that's right." Mrs. Mack stayed silent too long. "Do you have an alternative lined up, dear? I think that would be wise."

Drape had to agree. "Of course, Mrs. Mack. Thank you." After she hung up the phone she addressed Mother and Grandma. "Matt's been arrested for arson. He burned down all of Salvatore's property. I need to think of another best man for Sky."

"Why not let Sky worry about his best man?" Mother said.

Grandma nodded and Drape approved. She hadn't caused the problem, and she sure couldn't cure or control the outcome. "Good idea," Drape said. Proverbs 11:27 had started her day and read: "She that diligently seeth good procureth favor: but he that seeketh mischief, it shall come unto him."

* * *

Friday, May 31
Brighton Condo

After the dinner hour, Sky was happy to have Grandma instead of Drape open the door for him.

"Come in," Grandma said. "Do come in. We've been wondering who you will choose for your best man."

"Among other questions," Mother Taylor's frown telegraphed a lack of good will. Mother Taylor was ensconced on the living room couch, TV monitor on mute but her favorite nighttime soap already pulling her attention.

Grandma, on the other hand, continued to use a lemon-smelling spray cleaner on every surface in the kitchen: refrigerator door handle, stove-top hood, sink handles, even the ceramic pot-bellied-baker cookie jar.

"Combs called to tell me Matt has jumped bail." Sky looked around for Drape.

Drape came down the steps.

Sky was pulled to her beauty as if a magnet had been implanted right below his left collarbone. His ears tingled with embarrassment at his obvious attraction. Drape was wearing a soft lacy top over her jeans, but she would have been fashionable anywhere. Sky missed more than just her loveliness. He longed to connect with her brain, her wit, the whole person she was, which included an insane attachment to a murderer. He dropped his hand when it reached out for her.

Drape came closer and wiped a tear, which had initially escaped his notice, from his cheek. "I've missed you too. Never mind worrying, we are going to marry and we are going to be happy. What if I became a Republican, would you hate me then?"

Sky laughed with relief. "I would. Although, Mother would hate you more."

Drape put her arms around his neck. "Now we have to worry about Matt too?"

"We do," Sky said. "I love you."

"Thank the Lord." Drape smiled at him as if she knew all along he'd be back.

"Do you mind if Professor Chinich walks you down the aisle and Professor Clarke can be my best man?"

"That's fine," Drape said. "Pastor Nieman would like to speak to us again."

"Really," Sky said, not anxious to tread in dark waters so soon. "Well, let's make another appointment."

Mother Taylor had shut off the television and proceeded to bully Sky into the kitchen. "Young man, have you been spreading rumors you were not going to marry my daughter?"

"I did talk to Ike." Sky sat down on a new kitchen stool. "On the day I went to live with my folks."

"Get over here," Mother Taylor motioned for him to come to the wall phone, which he did. "You call everyone you spoke to, right now. The Bard would tell you, 'With what's un-real, thou co-active art.'"

"Mother," Drape said. "Sky doesn't have to call people in front of us."

"Yes, he does," Grandma said. "Hop to it, Sky."

Sky hoped Ike would be off somewhere with Burress, but she answered on the first ring. "I'm at our Brighton condo," he said to clue her into the sticky situation he found himself in.

"Drape's folks made you call?" Ike asked.

"They certainly did," Sky said, smiling at the three women surrounding him. "We want to be sure you'll show up as bridesmaid."

"Hey, that was never the problem, was it?" Ike laughed.

And Sky could hear her tell Mrs. Mack what a fool he was making of himself. "We love each other," Sky said to his audience. He didn't mind being bullied about for his own good.

"Good enough," Ike said. "Are your ears tingling?"

"They are," Sky admitted. "See you soon."

Mother Taylor had adjourned to the living room and Grandma headed upstairs.

"Want a piece of apple pie?" Drape asked. "Is your suitcase in the car?"

"Yes," Sky said following her into the dining room. "I was hoping you'd let me back in."

CHAPTER TWELVE

Saturday, June 1
Stone's Apartment

Ike and Drape agreed to help Mrs. Mack sort through Stone's belongings before she moved to her husband's apartment.

"Would it be easier, Stone," Mrs. Mack asked, "if you let the girls go through everything and just show you what's left?"

"What if I'm really attached to something they throw out?" The roots of Stone's hair were being sorely tested.

"We didn't have time to arrange a shower for you, but Grandma wanted you to have this." Drape handed Stone a black box containing Arpege perfume.

Stone smiled from ear to ear. "I love her perfume. Now Combs will think I smell good too."

"We could call Grandma to help us," Drape offered.

"No," Stone said. "Don't embarrass me even more. Go ahead. Why don't you throw what you want me to discard downstairs, and I'll put it in trash bags for Purple Heart? Then I'll pack what you decide to keep."

Ike was more reluctant to start the task than Drape thought she'd be. "Stone, are we going to lose you as a friend?"

"I promise," Stone said. "I have some sort of appropriateness problem. I know two friends when I see them. Besides, I've lost way too many people this year to question our friendships."

"Scant comfort," Ike said as she and Drape headed upstairs. "Nosey would be better at this. She was tough."

"Not tough enough," Drape said, shaken at the realization Nosey's bones were probably floating in UPS trucks somewhere between Ann

Arbor and Chicago. "Can you believe it, Salvatore said she climbed into the dermestids box to tease him?"

"So you think an unknown father is better than a murderer?" Ike asked.

Mrs. Mack defended Drape. "Now, Ike, don't make her feel worse than she does."

To begin, Mrs. Mack suggested they throw out all of Stone's multicolored pullover sweaters, keeping a few turtlenecks and matching cardigans. "Nothing infuriates me more than to see Stone pull off her sweater at the dinner table when she gets too warm."

Ike held up a clump of sports bras. "Should we pack a few support ones for her?"

Mrs. Mack blushed. "I did buy her seven, but how are we going to get her to wear one?"

"Let me try," Drape said. She hung her head over the upstairs banister. "Stone, you need to wear this under your wedding dress, okay?" She threw down the box and the three critiquers waited for Stone's reply.

"Well, okay," Stone said. "I'll put it on now. Should I come up?"

"No that's good," Drape said. "We'll see it when we're done."

Mrs. Mack wiped the perspiration from her forehead and whispered, "That went very well."

Ike wrapped the sports bras in with some ancient slips and flannel nightgowns and threw them down the steps. They all waited for Stone's reaction, but no sounds were forthcoming.

Drape laid all Stone's skirts on the bed. "I think she's kept every article of clothing she's ever owned since grade school. Has she shaved her legs yet?"

Mrs. Mack smiled. "I told her only men are allowed hairy legs on their wedding night. I bought her black tights in case she forgets to shave regularly."

"Good," Drape said, selecting three black skirts: one long, one short, and one with a flare skirt. The multicolored ones she ditched over the banister.

They heard a slight sigh from below, but no other comment.

After the purge, Stone only owned three decent dresses: one white, one black, and the yellow one for Drape's wedding. "Can't we find a proper wedding dress for her?"

Ike reached under the bed and pulled out a long garment box. "I tricked her into coming with me. She wants to surprise you but I didn't want you to worry. Wait until you see it on her."

Drape hugged Ike. "You are a good friend to her."

"We can count them on one hand now," Ike coughed, trying not to weep.

Mrs. Mack was going through a box of costume jewelry. "Will she sit still for us donating most of these to the Thrift Shop?"

"Let me go through the screw earrings," Drape said. "I can understand not wanting to have your ears pierced."

"Why, is it a religious thing?" Ike asked.

"I don't know," Drape said. "I guess it difficult to find people who are for abortion too."

"No one is ever for abortion," Mrs. Mack said. "But women do need to make responsible decisions, before pregnancy preferably."

When they finally allowed Stone back upstairs she seemed pleased with their decisions. "Mother never gave me any directions about dressing."

"Today is your big day," Mrs. Mack said. "Ike let the secret out and we all want to see you in your wedding dress. It's getting late."

* * *

St. Andrew's Episcopal Church

The ceremony was short and the audience few in number, but Stone Slager became Mrs. Lawrence Combs on a perfect June day. The dress she picked out with Ike sported a long straight skirt, with a slight train and the brocade bodice turned Stone into a bride of true elegance.

Mrs. Mack chose a charming tan suit to wear as matron of honor. Drape and Ike wore short chocolate brown dresses trimmed in tan piping. The flowers were yellow roses, Stone's mother's favorites. Sky was Combs's best man and Burress made a fine usher, towering over everyone.

Ike and Drape had spent a considerable amount of time with Stone, helping her move her belongings into Combs's larger house. Grandma helped arrange the brunch catered by Zingerman's for the reception at Combs's.

Mother had spent several hours with Stone at the Zingerman bakery to design a wedding cake decorated with yellow-rose icing.

Getting into the various cars to ride to Combs's apartment, Drape heard Salvatore's name when Sky asked Burress about finding the suspected culprit. "Have they found him?"

"No," Sky said. "He's still out there creating more havoc."

"What about Matt?" Combs asked.

Burress said, "I hope he keeps his wits about him. Bianco is a dangerous man."

Drape shook her head and Sky glared at her. Smiles she wanted smiles from her intended this close to their wedding. "I'm worried about Matt," Drape said to appease Sky.

"No you're not," Sky said. "You're afraid your precious father-figure will develop bullet holes!"

Drape refused to speak to Sky all the way to the Borders' parking structure across from Combs's apartment. But her anger wasn't subsiding. The reading of the day, Proverbs 12:4, didn't help: "A virtuous woman is a crown to her husband: but she that maketh ashamed is a rottenness in his bones."

When he opened the passenger door, which was in itself unusual, she couldn't stop her tongue. "Why do you think we have a justice system in this country?"

"Oh, to let tender-hearted liberals like you allow murderous criminals to run around killing innocents."

Sky's sarcasm crushed all of Drape's hopes for their future.

"You're an idiot." Drape crossed the street without looking and was nearly hit by a car taking the right-hand turn off Liberty Street too fast.

Sky rushed to her side. "You could have been killed."

"You'd probably find a way to blame that on Salvatore too," Drape said, sorry as soon as the words left her mouth. "Sorry, Sky. That car did scare me."

"Not enough," Sky said and stormed into Combs's apartment.

Drape stood outside until Stone opened the door. "Aren't you coming in?"

"We're fighting," Drape explained.

Grandma appeared at the door. "Get in here. Don't ruin Stone's reception. I'll get rid of Sky until you two come to your senses."

* * *

135

Combs's Apartment

Later Nikolai Burress brought Sky back into the apartment. "Courts are the last resort for civilized people. The closer you are to each other, the more disagreements can hurt."

Sky leaned against the closed door, ready to bolt back outside at the least provocation. Combs' second floor space reached up to white-painted rafters. The elongated windows were covered halfway up with white shutters. White wicker, blue padded furniture, giant ferns and blooming blue hydrangeas convinced Sky he had arrived at a botanical garden. The bedroom area was partitioned off with tall folding screens of white shutters.

Ike's stepmother moved closer to her husband on the love seat. "I don't believe people who love each other can cause each other harm intentionally."

Ike hooted, too loud for even Burress to ignore. "You know, I tell everyone you're my stepmother."

Mr. St. Claire waved his arm as if to ward off the angry words. "Why would you tell anyone that?"

"Because she's completely insane!" Ike strained to push Sky away from the door. "I need to get out of here."

Mrs. St. Claire stood and motioned to Ike's father. "We're leaving, Mr. Combs. I'm sure you and Stone will be very happy. I wouldn't advise you to have children though. They can be quite a stumbling block to happiness."

"How was I ever a stumbling block for you," Ike shouted. "You're the one who tried to kill my father. Tell them why we don't own steak knives."

"Ike," Mr. St. Claire said. "We don't need to rehash old business."

Burress touched Sky's shoulder. "Open the door, Sky. Ike's parents are not comfortable here."

Mrs. St. Claire glared at Burress. "Oh, Mr. High-and-Mighty. Think you're better than us? Think you will never have a life-and-death argument? Think again. Life is tough and when two people commit to live together for the rest of their lives, things can get sticky." She hung her head, but Sky could see the tears running down her cheeks. "Real sticky!"

Before Mr. St. Claire could shut the door, Ike's mother pushed it back open. "Ask your father why we were fighting, Ike. I dare you. Ask him."

Ike reached for her father's hand but he pulled away.

"No," he said. "Go ahead, tell her. You're the one who likes to let our life blow up in our faces. You can spread it on thick."

Smaller than anyone in the room, Mrs. St. Claire put her hands on her hips. "Ike's too-good-to-dust-my-floors father didn't want a third child. He insisted I have an abortion and I nearly went mad with grief!"

Only silence met her tirade. Mr. St. Claire didn't defend himself.

Ike turned her back on both of them.

Her brother, Stan, slipped out the door.

Sky stood outside until the three entered the parking structure across the street. When Sky finally shut the door, everyone inside was so quiet he thought he heard the St. Claire's car brake on the exit ramp.

Burress led him into the slant-roof kitchen. "I think that's what they call a Tiger Mom."

"Did she push Ike in school?" Sky asked. "Mother Taylor seems to have a hands-off policy for Drape, even though she's younger than the rest of the girls."

Drape entered the kitchen. "Is this the guy camp?" She came up to Sky, slid her arm around his waist.

"You're a good man, Sky." Burress excused himself.

Drape waited until they were alone to make up. "I'm marrying you. Even if I defend a murderer's right to life, I love and trust only *you* enough to marry. Only you, Sky."

Sky enfolded Drape as close to his chest as possible. Here was his wife-to-be, the girl he loved from the first time he watched her push her squeaky-clean, feathery hair behind her ears when she had been a student in his classroom.

* * *

When they returned to the living room, Ike was still facing the tall windows. Burress placed his hands on Ike's shoulders. She turned toward him and collapsed against his chest in tears. "See why I didn't call her my mother?"

137

Burress bent down on one knee. "I don't have the ring yet, Ike; but in front of all your friends, in spite of your family, will you please consent to be my wife?"

Drape screamed. "Congratulations!"

Ike laughed. "Hey, I haven't said yes yet."

"Say it," Sky said. "Say it!"

"Okay," Ike said. "I'll marry you, Nikolai Burress. Do we ever need to see those people again?"

"Only if they want to see their grandchildren," Burress said and hugged his fiancée.

Stone cut the cake and handed Ike the first piece. "This will bring both of you good luck like Larry and I enjoy."

Mrs. Mack scurried around taking pictures of Combs and Stone and making sure everyone ate enough.

Drape drew Ike aside, into the bathroom opposite the kitchen. Here the slanted roof and the vanity sink wall were mirrored. They both preened the back of their hair. Ike's thick black locks shone under the lighting, Drape's revealed red highlights among the brown strands. "I hope I'll be able to eat my wedding cake," Drape said. "Sky is such a bear about Salvatore Bianco."

"I'm not going to discuss your crazy behavior," Ike said.

"What do you mean?" Drape laughed. She didn't want to ruin Ike's happiness by challenging her. "Maybe the shifting ground in Washington made us both a little tipsy since birth."

Ike laughed then. "We should keep living in Ann Arbor. I always thought your home on Whidbey Island was less stable than the ground under our house in Bellevue."

* * *

Monday, June 3
Pastor Nieman's Study

"Did I miss you yesterday?" Pastor Nieman inquired.

"No, sorry," Drape said. "I didn't attend mass. Where is Mikey?"

"Sky, are you allergic to dog fur?" Pastor Nieman reached over the apartment's kitchen gate and pulled a much larger puppy to his chest.

"I'm not," Sky said. "I was upset the first time we met, about Salvatore Bianco."

Drape appreciated Sky's attempt at civility. He reached for Mikey, who snuggled up to him as easily as he had Pastor Nieman. Of course, everything wasn't clear about how she still felt about a man who admitted murdering more than one person she knew. But seeing the puppy matching her enthusiasm for the gentle man she intended to marry, helped her to reiterate her original trust in Sky's ability to open-heartedly love her.

"Is the air conditioning on too high?" Pastor Neiman asked. "Have you resolved your differences about the man?"

"No," Sky said. At the same time Drape said, "Yes."

"Sky," Pastor Nieman held up his hand to stop him from saying more. "Let's listen to why Drape thinks you are okay about Salvatore Bianco."

"Maybe I don't see his problem clearly enough," Drape said. She brushed off her jeans as she'd seen Mrs. Mack do a thousand times with the lap of her skirt. Proverbs 12:15 carried a double message: "The way of a fool is right in her own eyes, but she that hearkeneth not unto counsel is wise." Drape took a deep breath. "Neither of us want to give up the idea of marrying each other on June fifteenth." Drape hadn't meant the statement as a fishing exhibition; but Sky silence didn't encourage her. "I hope he doesn't have second thoughts about our happiness."

Sky's ears were turning red. "I'm never going to let go of you."

"Unless, what?" Pastor Nieman pursued.

Sky dropped his head. "It's too painful to talk about now."

Sitting hip to hip next to Sky, Drape touched Mikey's warm fur and then Sky's face. "I'm never going to let anyone or any outlandish idea of justice come between us."

Pastor Nieman stood up. Surprisingly he divested Sky of his furry companion. "Drape tell me how you view your situation with Salvatore Bianco at this point."

"I was wrong," Drape said. "I was looking for a father figure, and heaven knows there are plenty of people who could fill the empty place in my life." She pointed at Pastor Nieman. "You would be a good candidate, or Sky's father. He likes me too."

"But Salvatore ..." Sky couldn't continue.

"Yes," Drape said. "Salvatore's attentions muddied my thinking. He wasn't interested in being a friend. But I remember a story Mrs. Mack told us."

Sky waved his hand as if he didn't want to hear one more piece of wisdom from Drape's sorority mother.

"Continue," Pastor Nieman encouraged.

"Well, it seems one of our sorority sisters became a religious ... you know, a nun, who visited prisoners on death row. Illinois doesn't have a death penalty anymore. Anyway, she wrote a book about the soul of a convicted murderer—and Salvatore hasn't even been convicted yet."

"They would arrest him," Sky's jaw was developing a determined, icy set, "if they could lay their hands on him."

Drape directed the rest of her explanation to Pastor Nieman since Sky wasn't being the least bit receptive. "The soul of a man can contain a black, horrible spot, or maybe two or three; but the rest of his soul is as clean and loving as the day he was born."

"He would have been better born dead." Sky purposefully went into the kitchen and retrieved Mikey, who had been whining.

"Are you saying you need Sky to forgive Salvatore for killing your friends before you marry him?" Pastor Nieman watched Sky pet his puppy.

"No," Drape said. "I understand, Sky has never trusted the man and I don't expect I'll be able to forgive Salvatore, if he has ..."

"If?" Sky handed Mikey to the pastor and stormed out the door.

"Well that went well," Drape said, dissolving into a mess of tears and sniffing.

* * *

Brighton Condo

Sky's anger wouldn't let him enter the condo, so he sat on the concrete stoop, contemplating his next move and the flurry of daffodils nodding their heads in the plantings on each side of him.

Grandma opened the door. "The neighbors are going to think you're stalking Drape. Get in here. What went wrong?"

Sky hung his head and went inside. He sat down on the steps leading upstairs and held his head in his hands. "I don't know what to do."

"About?" Grandma asked.

"Bianco," Sky wanted to shout, but Grandma was such a kind woman. He felt the fight drain right out of him. "Drape still thinks he could be innocent."

"No, she doesn't." Grandma handed Sky a chocolate milk shake.

He thanked her and then asked, "Did you just make this for me?"

"I made it for myself," Grandma said, "but I made enough to share. Come into the living room and I'll give you a cup of coffee so you don't get a brain freeze."

Sky did as he was told. "I think my brain is frozen. I can't get around the idea of Salvatore Bianco still being in Drape's good graces."

"He's not." Grandma placed his milkshake on a coaster and handing him a cup of black coffee. "Christians are taught to forgive, but we're not stupid. She would never allow him around her again."

"Really?" Sky held the warm cup in his hands. "Maybe I should go back to Nieman's."

"Let Pastor Nieman teach Drape how to communicate her beliefs in a more positive way, Sky. She was wrong to upset you so close to the wedding."

"I'm afraid I've bungled everything." Sky studied Drape's grandmother. "How do you stay so serene?"

"My faith," Grandma said.

"Pastor Nieman asked me back in May if I believed in electricity." Sky finished his coffee. "Why did he ask me?"

"To prove you believe in something." Grandma got up, gathering the empty glass and coffee cup. "Would you like another cup?"

"I would," Sky said. He watched her head for the kitchen. Another thing he could easily believe in was the love Grandma possessed for her granddaughter. He got up and followed her into the kitchen. He experienced a feeling of wellbeing and actual warmth in her wake, as if the gentle surf of some southern sea washed over him. "Grandma," he said. "How did you first come to believe?"

Grandma laughed and handed him a fresh cup of coffee. "When I was about your age, I met my husband. He was a lot older than me. I was terrified of life, of him, of what the world was all about. As I walked down the aisle on my wedding day, I said the AA Third Step Prayer. At this late date I don't remember why; probably someone I knew had a parent in AA, or maybe my husband's family. He never drank. Well anyway, I prayed for the first time in my adult life."

"What was the prayer?" Sky asked intrigued and ready to find a serene emotional life.

Grandma bowed her head. "Lord, I offer you my life and my will to do with or to build with whatever is Your will. Grant me victory over my present difficulties so that I may bear witness to those I am trying to help of Your power, Your love, and Your glory."

"And did He?" Sky asked.

"Oh yes," Grandma said. "I conquered my fears, I married Richard, I gave birth, and I live a grateful life."

'I don't believe in a personal god."

"Why not?" Grandma poured herself a cup of coffee, adding cream and sugar. "You believe He created the world?"

"I do," Sky said. "My parents don't. But everything is so precise in mathematics, so elegant and pure, the solutions I mean. There had to be an initial intelligent plan. We don't understand it all; but the answers are there waiting for our discovery."

"Why couldn't a god that grand, that all-encompassing hold each of us in the palm of His hand, measure each of our sighs, count the feathers on every bird?"

"I wish I had your gift of faith," Sky said.

"The Lord is only waiting for one thing from you," Grandma said.

"What's that?"

"For you to ask," Grandma said. "He promised if you knocked, He would answer."

"I do love Drape, you know," Sky felt pitifully stupid.

"She knows," Grandma said, "And that's a 'concreteful fact' according to Sugarman, Rodriquez."

"Cool," Sky said finally able to relax, but not yet ready to offer a petition to a god who might not answer. "I am a grateful person," Sky said, not knowing exactly to whom he was grateful. Then he realized. "I left Drape in Ann Arbor without a car. Will you call Pastor Nieman? Tell him I'll be there in twenty minutes—and I'm sorry."

* * *

Ann Arbor Streets

After Sky stormed out of Pastor Nieman's, Drape wandered around the third floor of the parking garage off Williams Street for fifteen minutes before she realized Sky had driven off without her. Taxis were always available in front of the Student Union, which was only six blocks away. Her anger would be gone by the time she got in the cab. How long would it take Sky to cool off? Maybe he hadn't even gone back to the condo. As she walked down Williams toward the balanced cube structure, next to the Union, she looked around for Sky's van to see if he might have waited for her on a side street.

Salvatore Bianco called to her from a few steps behind. Burress was right, he was still stalking her.

"Salvatore," she said, stiff-arming him as he sought to embrace her. "There's an arrest warrant out for you."

He laughed. "How do you like my new shoes?"

Drape blinked. His tennis shoes didn't match. "Where's your car?"

"I ditched it," he said.

"Grandma will make sure you have a good attorney, Salvatore." Drape's head was spinning. Where were the police when you needed them? "Let's check you in at the Campus Inn."

"Good idea," Salvatore said turning north as they walked hand-in-hand.

As they reached State Street, Drape changed her mind. "Mother has influence at the League. You could wait in the foyer, while I make arrangements."

"That's okay," Salvatore said. "I'll go with you. You can tell them I'm your Dutch uncle."

Drape was amazed she could chuckle in spite of being terrified. She checked her watch as they crossed North University. Nearly eight o'clock, and the daylight helped. He wouldn't hurt her with all these people milling about, would he?

"Were you wearing a wire when we talked at your condo?" Salvatore pulled her to his side.

"I was," Drape admitted. "They insisted you were guilty."

"I do love you, Drape," Salvatore said it with sincerity, and Drape believed him.

"We'll make sure they treat you okay," she said, as he opened the League's heavy entrance door. She walked toward the check-in desk. Surely everyone knew Salvatore Bianco was a dangerous man, but the tall, beefy male clerk smiled a rehearsed welcome as she signed Salvatore's name to the register.

Salvatore leaned over her shoulder. "Room 205?"

Drape didn't have a chance to write, "Help, Call the Police." Instead she smiled and led Salvatore toward the steps.

"Let's take the elevator," Salvatore said. "I'm tired."

Drape didn't want to be alone with him in the elevator, but she didn't know how to run away or make a scene.

Once the door closed and the elevator began to move, Salvatore hit the stop button. "We need to talk," he said.

Drape realized he hadn't bathed, probably for days. "We should have ordered room service," she said, still able to smile at this monster who had already killed two of her sorority sisters.

CHAPTER THIRTEEN

Michigan League Elevator

Drape leaned against the wall opposite Salvatore Bianco. She could feel an icy cold creep up her legs from the floor. "It's cold in here," she said. "Sky and I just finished our second visit with Pastor Nieman. His air conditioning wasn't as chilling."

Salvatore smiled. "It's fear."

"Should I be afraid?" Drape kept her eyes steady but the cold made her hug her arms, and she slid down the wall. She let go of her arms long enough to hug her knees to her chest.

Salvatore sat down too. "I want to explain to someone."

"I'm a good listener," Drape said. She found it difficult to talk because her teeth wanted to start chattering from the chill.

Salvatore nodded. He got up and took off a light wind-jacket, draping it over her knees. His warmth from the jacket helped, but the smell was revolting. She breathed through her mouth, and she sounded like a stuttering child. "Th-th-thanks."

After he sat down opposite her, he said, "Stone's mother was the first. She wouldn't believe I loved her. Time after time I drove up to Evanston to plead through her apartment door. But no, she was too good to let me in. As a last resort, I broke in through the fire escape window."

Salvatore wasn't looking at her anymore. Drape felt released from the riveting gaze of a hungry snake. Her options were few. She'd stopped shivering. *Lord,* she prayed, *Your will be done.* Somehow it helped to remember she was not entirely alone with an insane person.

145

"I didn't really kill her," Salvatore said intent on his dirty fingernails. "I hugged her to my chest to keep her quiet. Once and a while, I'd release her head long enough to look into her beautiful face, but she'd take a breath and start to yell."

Salvatore smiled, looking at Drape as if he expected her to approve. Then he shrugged and studied the palm of his left hand. "She's the only one I shipped to Ann Arbor."

Staggered by her own courage, Drape asked. "And Nosey?"

"A hateful person," Salvatore said. "She tricked me into believing Blacky wanted to be my lover." He was still scrutinizing his fingers as if someone had sewn Frankenstein's hands to his wrists. "I'm probably insane."

"We can find you a good defense lawyer," Drape said.

"I left Nosey's bones at the Field Museum. She didn't deserve to return to Ann Arbor, but her bones were pure. Dead meat has a revolting smell, but I never minded handling their untainted bones. I liked owning their bones." Salvatore stood up and reached for her hands, but Drape stayed on the floor.

"The Schultz family came up to Ann Arbor for Blacky's funeral." Drape liked it better when Salvatore was seated. She motioned for him to sit back down, and he obeyed.

"Matt was the worst," Salvatore said. "Did you know he burned down my home and my apartment?"

"They arrested him," Drape said, trying to sound sympathetic.

"One angry man," Salvatore said, reevaluating his fingers, again. "I thought you all might appreciate Blacky's arrangement, such a beauty. I couldn't mar her flesh to get at her bones."

"Is Matt okay?" Drape asked. "He's Sky's best man."

"There's not going to be a wedding, if I can help it," Salvatore said. He smiled in her direction. "You love me, don't you?"

"I did think of you as a friend," Drape admitted.

"But not now." Salvatore seemed to accept the inevitable fact. "You couldn't love a monster now."

"You're not a monster," Drape hoped.

Salvatore ran his hands through his beautiful hair. "I'm not sure. Maybe my brain is different than it should be. I don't think it's normal to search for the bones in people's bodies while they're still alive. When I see overweight people, I feel so sorry for their bones. Young women, slim ones, are so intriguing. They only have a thin encasement of flesh on their framework. Their bones are really marvelous—elbows sticking out, knees a bit knobby. I love the bones, even after they're dead."

Drape was freaking out. Her own bones started to shudder. So he was crazy all along, and she hadn't known it. That anonymous sperm bank looked cozy from this angle.

"I took Matt for a ride in his van." Salvatore smiled but looked toward the doors of the unmoving elevator, as if knowing she couldn't return his smile. "I wanted to explain to him how I'd became the person I am. Blacky was so beautiful. No wonder he loved her. He didn't even mention the flowers I'd picked for her. He didn't want to go with me, of course, so I knocked him out and taped his mouth shut with see-through packing tape, in case someone looked through the passenger window. I even buckled his seat belt after I'd taped his hands behind his back and his shoes together."

Drape hadn't made a sound, but Salvatore checked to see if she was attentive.

"I drove him out to St. Charles, to the Boys' Home where I lived from the time I was twelve until I was fourteen." Salvatore's face softened for a moment. "When we were out in the fields the wind could hit us from all four directions at the same time." As his memory shifted to the present time, Salvatore's expression darkened. "I explained to Matt the only reason they let me out was because I nearly died after they punished me."

"What did they reprimand you for?" Drape asked because Salvatore had gotten too quiet for too long. His face was turning grey, not red, as his inner fury increased.

"Reprimand?" Salvatore stared at the door, unable to face her. "After I hit a kid in the head with a shovel when he tried to touch my private parts, the guards held me upside down in the sewage drain." Salvatore smiled a gruesome, lopsided smile. "Everyone loves my white hair, but that's how I got it—from all the antibiotics they fed me to fend off the infections in my eyes, and ears and mouth."

"Oh, Salvatore," Drape's tears were releasing down her cheeks.

"That wasn't the worst," Salvatore said. "I enlightened Matt. My mother used to tell me it cost her money just for me to wake up in the morning. I was hustling on the streets of Chicago by the time I was ten."

"Where's Matt now?" Drape asked, mostly to change the subject.

"He didn't know I had a gun with me. I think he thought I would just leave him in his van to explain to everyone why I'd murdered people. He didn't suffer. I shot him from behind the van, through the window into the back of his head." Salvatore tapped the floor to get Drape's attention. "I left the van with the gun in the driver's seat at the Boys' Home. I made sure Matt didn't have a pulse."

"Are you going to turn yourself in now?" Drape asked. "The Lord will forgive you."

"No, I never believed in a god. I knew you did and I didn't want your belief to be a stumbling block to loving me." Salvatore pulled on his left ear, as if refusing to listen to more evil advice. "I just wanted to let you know how everything went down."

"I understand," was all Drape could think to say.

"I know," Salvatore said. Then he stood up and pushed the elevator button, stepping out on the League's second floor. "See you."

Drape stayed on the floor as the elevator doors closed. She got up and pushed the button for the first floor. The doors closed before she realized Salvatore had left his jacket with her.

When the elevator doors opened on the first floor, a gang of policeman grabbed her. A thousand questions rained down on her.

"Second floor," she managed.

Three policemen ran up the stairs while three more got in the elevator.

The male receptionist helped her stand as they watched the old dial move as the elevator rose. "Come into the back room, where you'll be safe. The cops said they called your family and two detectives. There's an FBI agent involved?"

"There is," Drape said. "So you did recognize Salvatore?"

"I did, but I didn't know what to do," the guy said. "Did he hurt you?"

"No," Drape said. "Salvatore would never hurt me. Although, he is insane."

* * *

Brighton Condo

Grandma had answered the kitchen phone for Sky. She caught him before he was halfway down the front walk to his van.

Back inside, Sky took the phone as Grandma sat down too hard on the kitchen stool. Burress' voice was urgent. "Come back to Ann Arbor. Salvatore has Drape in the Michigan League elevator."

"She'll be all right." He said more to himself than to her grandmother.

The drive down Route 23 was torture. He didn't want to kill anyone, but the dial read 85 before he could concentrate enough to wonder why everyone was driving so slowly. When he got off at the Main Street exit, he reduced his speed, but driving fifty miles an hour down Huron did afford him green lights all the way past Rackham. When he turned into the League's driveway, he checked his watch. The sun was starting to set.

Once in the Michigan League, the sight of Drape calmed him. She was sitting in the doorway of a room behind the reception desk with a blanket over her shoulders.

Policemen were everywhere.

"Did he hurt you?" Sky asked, when the crowd of officials finally listened to Burress and Combs long enough to identify Sky as a friend.

"Of course not," Drape said.

Sky didn't care if she hated him for asking, his relief included a rush of affection for his intended. "Forgive me, Drape. Please, I love you."

"He's insane," she said before dissolving in tears into his arms.

* * *

Burress, Combs and a Washtenaw Sheriff interrogated Drape in the back room of the League. Sky refused to let her answer their questions alone. She wondered if she was hurting his hand which she held tightly in her lap. "I don't know where he is," she'd said several times. "He admitted killing Mrs. Slager, Nosey, Blacky, and Matt. You'll find Matt's body in his van in St. Charles. I don't know where the Boys' Home is located there."

"The place is still open, but they don't make the boys farm anymore," the Washtenaw Sheriff said. He was slimmer than Drape thought sheriffs were supposed to be. Maybe because of Ann Arbor's health-conscious culture, he ate yogurt instead of donuts.

Burress was busy on his phone, so Combs asked, "Did he give you any other information about Nosey's body?"

"It's in the Field Museum collection." The enormity of Salvatore's crimes swamped Drape's mind. "How could one human being wreak so much destruction?"

Sky's voice shook with emotion, "You're safe, Drape, you're not in any danger now."

Combs coughed. "Sky we haven't apprehended him. I'm requesting two uniformed policemen guard both of you until he's behind bars."

"No problem," the sheriff said.

Drape understood. "Sky, they're going to use us as bait."

"You don't want to delay our wedding, do you?" Sky asked.

She did, but Sky was in such a pitiful state she couldn't ask him to change their plans. Although, Drape could say that Combs and Burress thought delaying the marriage ceremony was a great idea. "Of course not," she said, trying vainly to smile at the two detectives. But when she looked at the sheriff's uniform, she broke down. Salvatore was surely going to be harmed by someone.

* * *

Saturday, June 8
Henderson Household, Lansing

"Our third meal," Jim Henderson began. "Hasn't Geraldine outdone herself this time?"

Sitting next to his mother, Sky felt the tops of his ears tingling.

Drape smiled at him from the opposite end of the table, next to his father, to acknowledge Sky's embarrassment.

Sky complimented his mother too. "You love to have us all here, don't you?"

"Because I'm a control freak." Geraldine laughed at her own joke. "The weather is so lovely, you'd think I arranged it too. However, my neighbors will be buzzing about the police car escort your fiancée arrived with."

Burress ignored her reference to the danger lurking outside. "One of the reasons I love warmer weather is strictly selfish." He touched Ike's apricot-colored blouse. "Women reveal more of their loveliness. And we're not aware Bianco knows your address."

Directly across the table, Mother Taylor stared at Sky as if she expected an acknowledgement of their safety from him. But he was distracted because at the other end of the table, Drape was indeed lovely in a strapless blue-flowered frock of some thin material Sky longed to touch.

Mother Taylor said, "Your menu is superb for the season. Cold cucumber soup and the standing rib roast smells delicious."

Professor Chinich, sitting between Combs and Drape's grandmother, let out a loud guffaw. "Sorry. I get it, lamb. But this poor fellow won't be leaping upon any lawn."

Grandma stroked his arm. "Isn't he grand? After Drape's wedding, Paul is going to join me in Fort Lauderdale."

Sky took a minute to realize Professor Chinich's first name was Paul. He remembered Drape had mentioned Chinich was sweet on her grandmother. Now they were going to be living together, without benefit of marriage?

Chinich cleared up any lingering thoughts about inappropriateness. "At our age, marriage is rather archaic, since we'll be living together as brother and sister."

Mother Taylor's face changed expression four or five times during the exchange. "Mother," she said, "my bridge partners have deserted me in Vero Beach. One man died, the other is going senile, and my female partner is no longer interested in seeking new partners just because the males quit. Could I join you in Fort Lauderdale, until I find a place of my own down there?"

Drape clapped her hands. "I'd feel so much better, Grandma. I hate thinking of you two living in different cities. Didn't you miss Mother?"

Grandma smiled. "I did miss your mother, but you know how addicted she was to her bridge game. And I so love the city's waterways in Fort Lauderdale. It's like living in a freshly built Venice, but with trees."

Leave it to Stone to crash their good mood. "Mother never missed me after I left for college. I think she was relieved to sell our house in Springfield and move to Chicago."

Mrs. Mack, always the paragon of politeness, turned the conversation to a brighter subject. "Your mother missed getting to know your husband."

"Mrs. Slager would have changed your name back to Shelby." Combs put his arm around the back of Stone's chair and tugged at the French braid her unruly hair had been tamed into. "If she'd witnessed your transformation."

Ike agreed. "You've pushed past all your reticence, Stone. Shall we christen you Shelby?

Stone raised her wine glass. "Lord, hereby find Shelby, your witness and servant."

They all raised their glasses in concert. "To Shelby!"

Sky's mother, a less than perfect hostess, said, "Religion is not welcome in our house."

"But peaceful believers are," Jim Henderson said rather loudly.

"Remember when we toasted at the last meal?" Sky asked.

"Back in March, eons ago, beautiful Blacky Schultz raised her glass," Drape said, raising her own again.

Sky's father waited until everyone had raised glasses. "To Life!"

* * *

Drape felt a surge of affection for her intended father-in-law. "They say religion is for those who fear damnation and spiritual life is for those who have been there."

Combs added, "You have certainly gone through a terrible time."

Mother said, "I never understood the victims of violence when I volunteered at an Abuse Center on Whidbey Island."

Drape remembered something. "Didn't they ask you to leave?"

"They did," Mother said. "Before wife abuse was made a crime against the state, women would stop prosecution of their husbands. Now the state pursues each case. Back then I told a woman with children, who we took in for the night, while the police allowed her drunken husband to remain at home, that the next time he fell asleep she should even the score with her iron skillet. The Center told me I needed to wait for the victim to come up with her own solution."

Ike said quietly, "I knew immediately after I met Salvatore Bianco there wasn't an appropriate bone in his body."

Drape didn't feel like disclosing Salvatore's fixation with bones. "How did you know?" she asked. "I just thought he was a warm, handsome older guy, my father figure in disguise."

The newly named Shelby said, "I bet that sperm bank your mother used looks pretty good now."

"Sperm bank?" Sky's mother asked.

"I'll explain later," Sky said.

Burress returned to Mother Taylor's subject. "The FBI has made studies of victim profiles. They are not very helpful. Of course, violent backgrounds lead some women to view violent men as normal, but just as many develop an early warning system. The authorities no longer disregard calls from frightened women. We even have a special method for checking out concerns from mothers. It's called a well-being search. Mothers often know when something is going wrong with their offspring in cities all the way across the country. Mothers in California call about daughters in Brooklyn. And women in Florida call about children in school in Minnesota. We don't wait for twenty-four hours to pass anymore. We check on their concerns."

Ike said, "We don't know Nosey's motivation, or her parentage. We kidded she was hatched."

"She was aggressive," Drape said. "It served her professional goals."

Mrs. Mack coughed politely. "I did get to know Nosey's background. I don't know if you knew she had a drinking problem. I took her to her first AA meeting. Afterwards, she began to trust me, probably because I kept her recovery a secret. Her father never controlled his temper. He was dyslexic, apparently fairly intelligent but unschooled. They moved to different farms every year because he found it difficult to work for people. Trying to hide the fact he couldn't read must have caused most of his stress. Nosey hid a razor strap he punished them with under a floorboard when they moved when she was about ten."

Drape put her fork down. "We didn't know."

"The violence went back generations in her family," Mrs. Mack said. "The stories aren't very palatable for dinner conversation."

"Oh for Pete's sake," Ike said. "Tell us. I'm ashamed we didn't even hold a wake for Nosey. Are her parents still alive?"

"I did contact her mother," Mrs. Mack said. "Her father passed away from a stroke when he was quite young. He was beaten by his father on their farm. There were nine children. He was the oldest. I remember their names because they were so strange. He was Denzle Udale. His brothers were called Orlando, Lloyd, J.D. and Darrell. The sisters were Vernita, Florence and Jessie." Mrs. Mack seemed to forget her worries about appropriate rules for dinner dialogue. "His father drank too much and threatened suicide often, scaring the children and his redheaded wife. Maybe that's why Nosey was so attracted to redheaded Blacky. Sorry, so one time Nosey's grandfather was digging, you know, for a new outhouse placement. Well, Denzle was watching and Israel, that was his name, threw a shovel of dirt at his son. The boy moved away and his dad threw another shovel right at him. Nosey says she remembered the look on her father's face as he told the story of how much his father hated him, all the children and farming. Apparently the grandmother owned the land."

"So Nosey couldn't recognize Bianco was violent," Ike said.

"What's my excuse?" Drape asked.

Grandma pointed an impolite finger at her mother. "Your mother's crazy answer to a lack of suitable courting men caused your ridiculous quest for a father figure. It blinded you to his insanity."

"He was always so good to me," Drape said.

Mother said, "Don't listen to your grandmother. I dated two murderers, Drape. One had served time for a jealous rage when he was in his twenties. I met him when he was sixty. His emotions were all deadened. I guess because he was afraid of feelings by then. The other man, a former drug addict, arranged for all the bones to be broken in a snitch who sent him to prison for theft. He'd turned his life around after his prison term and was helping ex-cons find employment. Murder has no statutory limit for prosecution, but by the time I realized I should have turned him in, he'd died."

Drape had never heard either story before. "Did you know Salvatore was violent?"

"I didn't," her mother admitted. "I just didn't like him. If my mother hadn't been praying for me all the years I was so independent and adventuresome, I don't know if I would have survived."

"You did just fine," Grandma said. "Did you know your mother was thrown out of prison, Drape?"

"What?" half the table joined in.

"I volunteered at a woman's prison with a twelve-step program," Mother said. "I brought in library books and realized the girls didn't have stationary, so one night I brought in note cards, but I put stamps on the envelopes. Apparently, those are regarded as banned, because the girls trade them around. And they wouldn't let me back in. I was always more afraid of the mean guards than of the women. Half of them are there for murder, from accidents when they were drunk, and the other half for defending their children from abusive husbands."

Geraldine said, "I volunteer at a preschool program. Maybe you could find one in Fort Lauderdale."

"Good idea," Mother said. "I'll look into it."

Grandma said, "Society is changing so rapidly. The FBI recognizes precognition of mothers to their children's welfare, while at the same time therapists are advising us not to smother our children with affection or controlling behavior. I don't know how young people can decide how to raise children."

Sky said, "Did I tell you I had a dream Valentine's Day after I'd moved Drape's belongings to Brighton?" No one answered, so Sky went on. "Mother, Mother Taylor and Grandma were sitting behind a long table. Drape and I came up with several names and you all approved, Ann and Ruth for the girls and Sam and Ted for the boys."

"Now all we have to do is make the babies," Drape said. She realized the other guests were embarrassed, so she added. "My dress fitting went perfectly this morning. I'll look like a dream to you, Sky."

"You always appear as if you stepped right out of Heaven's door," Sky rhapsodized.

* * *

As Mrs. Henderson passed around Boston cream pie, Larry Combs moved the topic to safer ground. "Did I hear you two are honeymooning in Europe?"

"They are," Sky's mother-in-law said.

"We have June, July and August," Sky said.

Drape said, "I haven't had time to make arrangements anywhere."

Grandma said, "I'll contact my travel agent and your itinerary could be ready for your wedding present. Where do you want to travel?"

"Florence and Mont-St-Michel," Drape said.

"I want to use the Chunnel," Sky said, "And see Ireland and England, Stonehenge and Bath."

"Will you have time to visit Jerusalem?" Shelby asked.

Combs leaned over and kissed his new bride. "We need a honeymoon too. Grandma Taylor, could you ask your agent to arrange a trip to the Holy Land?"

* * *

When the party broke up, Combs and Burress conferred with the uniformed policemen stationed in front of the house.

"Street was pretty empty," the oldest officer said. "No Lincoln passed by and no pedestrians. Except for a dark haired guy with a poodle. I watched until he went inside the house next door. Funny I didn't see him leave to take the dog for a walk and I've been out here for a long time."

Burress said, "Let's go over and introduce ourselves."

Combs agreed and told Jim Henderson to make some excuse to keep everyone inside until they returned. "Tell them we need to clear the area."

After knocking for several minutes, they heard a muffled cry inside. The two policemen put their shoulders to the entrance, which broke the molding off the door. Inside, the neighbors had been tied up with duct tape. A poodle was urinating on the hall stairs.

"He didn't take anything," the older house owner said. "He apologized for frightening us and shut off all the lights."

His wife said, "He just kept looking across the street at the Henderson's dinner party. Left about a half-hour ago."

Combs and Burress arranged for the front door to be fixed. They also called to have the poodle picked up by the pound for identification. Then they transmitted the new description of Bianco with his hair dyed to the FBI and the sheriff's office before returning to give the upsetting news to Drape and Sky.

Sky started yelling at them for not capturing Bianco. His father finally got him to calm down.

Grandma Taylor asked if they were safer in the Brighton Condo.

Burress promised the officers would be replaced with a fresh crew to keep watch throughout the night. "Drape, unfortunately, is his stalking prey. Do you own a gun?"

"Of course not," Drape said. "Salvatore isn't armed, is he?"

Combs hoped he was calming everyone down without giving the impression they didn't need to take precautions. "Bianco left his gun in the van with Matt. He hasn't tried to harm Drape."

"Yet!" Sky seemed ready to knock the stuffing out of someone.

"Stay with your folks until the wedding, Sky." Drape could see Sky was more of a danger to himself than a help to anyone else. "Shelby and Combs will use the master bedroom until we're safely married and Salvatore either gives up or is captured."

Burress agreed. "Sky, you are not helping matters. Drape will be safer if you stay in Lansing."

"I don't agree," Sky said.

"Never mind, darling," Mother Henderson said. "We'll listen to the authorities. They do know their business."

After they shut the door on the Henderson's, Drape said to Combs, "Nice how future mother-in-laws rule."

Combs had to laugh. "Definitely. We will keep you protected, Drape."

Drape hugged him. "I know you're going to give it your best. I can't ask for more. You know I'll be praying for your safety too."

* * *

Saturday, June 15
Brighton Condo

"When did I age?" Drape asked the vanity mirror in the master bedroom. Ike and Shelby both groaned.

Mrs. Mack said, "You are as beautiful as the first day you opened the sorority's front door."

Drape touched the corner of her drooping mouth. "Am I ever going to laugh again?"

"Give it a break," Ike said.

Shelby added, "Self-pity is not becoming."

Drape's mirror's image didn't change. She did pity the selfish girl in the mirror who had lost any hope of finding a loving father figure to replace the sperm-bank parent she would never know. Proverbs 12:25: "Heaviness in the heart of a woman maketh it stoop, but a good word maketh it glad." Salvatore—now with dark hair—was out there somewhere hiding from the police. She wondered if she'd even recognize him. "Poor thing," Drape said.

Shelby turned her away from the mirror. "It's your wedding day, Curtain."

"Curtain?" Drape started to cry. "Why are you calling me Curtain?"

"Straighten up." Ike shook Drape's shoulders. "Don't you love Sky?"

"I do," Drape said, laughing nervously. "I guess I'm rehearsing my response."

So this was maturity at age twenty. It didn't feel good. Drape stepped away from her vanity and opened the windows on each side of it. A light breeze cooled the stuffy room. Was Salvatore watching her windows even now? She sat back down and resurveyed her gloomy face. Where was the happiness she was supposed to be feeling? She remembered spinning like a happy child in Gallup Park in front of Salvatore. "Sky loves me," she said more to hear it herself than to convince her friends. What else did she need on what was supposed to be the most blissful day of her life?

"I was scared on my wedding day," Shelby admitted.

"I'm not frightened," Drape said. "I just don't feel as happy as I thought brides did on their wedding day."

"You are still grieving for our friends," Ike said.

Drape concurred. Shelby's yellow bridesmaid dress wasn't as cheerful as she remembered on the day they'd purchased it and Ike's light blue one could almost be grey. "They buried Blacky in her emerald bridesmaid dress."

"Should I ask your mother and grandmother to join us?" Mrs. Mack asked.

"No." Drape collected her wits. "It's bad enough I'm affecting your moods with my negative sway."

"Hey," Ike said, "I'm responsible for my own feelings. And right now I'd like to slap you silly before I bring out your dress." Ike towered over Drape. "You're just sulking because your big hero turned out to be a dreadful creep."

"Take it easy, Ike," Shelby said. "She still feels for the guy."

Ike shook her head. "You're as crazy as he is, Drape."

"I am not," Drape said. "Shelby's right I still feel some sympathy for his insanity, but I miss Blacky and Matt, even Nosey, too much to feel anything but anger toward him."

"About time," Ike said. "Are you going to get married and start a family or continue this pity party?"

"I'm going to marry Sky." Drape stood up. "Now go get my dress so I can drip tears on it all the way down the aisle."

Ike turned toward the closet and then came back and embraced Drape. "I promise you Sky will always love you."

Shelby held out a blue velvet box. "Your grandmother said to call her up when you're ready to open this."

"I can't wait," Drape said. "Grandma, come in."

Grandma and Mother must have been standing in the hall listening. "Oh I wanted to wait until you had your dress on," Grandma said.

"Never mind, Mother," Mother said. "Let her open the box."

Drape took the light blue box from Shelby. Inside was a long string of pearls.

"They'll match the ones on your dress," Grandma said.

"Oh they're beautiful," the three girls chimed in and laughed.

"She wore them on her wedding day," Mother said.

"And you're the first person to wear them on her wedding day since—too many years ago to count," Grandma said, getting a bit misty around the eyes.

Mother said, "Now they belong to you, Drape."

Drape was astonished by the pearls but mainly because of what her mother had just said. "Mother, that's the first time you have ever used my nickname."

Mother hugged her. "You earned it, Drape. Now drape those pearls around your beautiful neck."

Drape didn't want to cry but as far as she could remember, her mother had never mentioned she thought she was anything but plain. "I'll never understand either of you."

Grandma was the first to regain her composure. "Mark Twain says we all have a universe behind our buttons, in this case our pearls."

"I heard the other day that the universe is still expanding from the Big Bang," Shelby said. "The moon is moving away from the earth, slowing it down actually. I wonder if it will affect the tides or menstrual cycles."

Mother said, "And here we three Taylor women are getting ready to move away from each other, again."

Drape hugged the two of them. "You were never closer to my heart than now."

CHAPTER FOURTEEN

St. Andrew's Episcopal Church

In front of the altar, Sky stood next to Professor Clarke, who looked like an international diplomat in his gray tuxedo. Sky smiled at Grandma. Her pink suit offset the bright blue suit of Mother Taylor on her right and the pale green suit of Mrs. Mack, seated on her left. He checked the open door of the church but Drape was nowhere in sight. Anxious about Salvatore's whereabouts he studied the aisles and side entrances.

Two uniformed policemen were stationed at each door. Salvatore Bianco wasn't going to stop the wedding if the officials had anything to say about it. For a second, Sky thought he could hear gunfire; but he chalked it up to the state of his nerves. He checked his watch. Eleven o'clock.

Larry Combs was whispering to the FBI agent in the narthex.

Combs had shed his jeans and tennis shoes, but Sky still recognized him in his tailored navy-blue suit. Both their faces were hidden because of the sunshine glaring behind them, but their rigid stances during the conversation did not bode well.

Burress hurriedly walked down the side aisle and up the two steps leading to the altar. "We found Matt's body where Salvatore said it would be. They still haven't apprehended him."

Sky nodded and Burress returned to his ushering duties.

Professor Clarke said, "I've never known anyone to marry in the midst of this whirlwind of violence. How are you doing?"

"Shaky," Sky said. "I'm sure of only one thing."

"What's that," Professor Clarke asked.

"I'm going to marry the love of my life," Sky said, chuckling nervously. "If she ever arrives."

He no longer cared what Drape thought of Salvatore's chances once he'd been arrested for the three—no, four!—murders. They could hang him or send him to a life-long stay in a crazy bin. Sky only wanted to claim his bride above the fray, whisk her off to become his life-long companion. Her former wit and laughter had been dampened by the recent tragedies, but in time life and her belief system would revive her true spirit. Time was what he was intent on promising; all the time she would ever need by his side.

The church was rapidly filling with Drape's classmates and Sky's colleagues from both Michigan universities.

Professor Clarke said, "Maybe you should pray. I know you're not a believer, but this might be the time to act as if you are."

Sky stared at his best man. Here was a man of science giving into all the superstitions connected to the place. The church's shape of an overturned boat or the pinnacles of trees never inspired him to seek the source of his fiancée's belief. "This is probably as close as I'm going to get to a foxhole."

"Do you know how to pray?" Professor Clarke asked.

"I don't, do you?" Sky said, just to humor him.

"Bow your head," Professor Clarke said. "If you can't repeat the words out loud, say them in your soul."

"As if I believe?" Sky asked. He remembered AA people often said that, or was it Alanon?

Professor Clarke nodded and bowed his head. "Please, Lord of the Universe, accept our prayer. Bless this union, which these two people have summoned the courage to enter in to despite the furies surrounding them."

Aloud Sky added, "Thy will be done."

"Good job," Professor Clarke said.

* * *

As Drape picked up the front of her dress to mount the church steps, she remembered she wanted the full skirt and petticoats of her wedding gown to represent the hoop skirts of the Civil War when St. Andrew's was built. Now she was under armed guards as if a war was still raging because some maniac wanted to stop her wedding. She heard gunfire downtown somewhere and hoped it was simply a car backfiring.

A warm breeze lifted the back of her lace veil as she stepped through the open doors. Then, a burst of joy escaped her soul. Now, here was the emotion she'd anticipated. '*Thank you, Lord,*' she prayed.

Professor Chinich looked regal as he offered his arm. "The happy bride arrives," he said.

Ike gave her the bouquet of lilies-of-the-valley. "Now there's my delightful friend."

Shelby looked back once and smiled, before heading down the aisle toward Sky.

The policemen on each side of the door both grinned at Drape. She winked at them and followed Ike down the white satin runner. Mrs. Mack or someone had decorated the church aisles with the planned evergreen swags and lilies, even though blood had been shed from her absent bridesmaids. Poor misguided Nosey Petersen and beautiful redheaded Blacky Schultz and her constant lover, Matt North, had gone down celestial avenues, under the hand of a man she'd trusted. Drape shook her head. The future awaited her, and she couldn't change the past.

Sorority sisters who attended her shower were in attendance. Seated between Professors Foster and Leland, Rose Grace Warner wore a light blue lacey dress with a matching summer hat.

In the row across from them, the Biblical sisters Mary and Martha, Mary Alice Walker, and Margaret O'Malley were still gossiping about Rose Grace's draw on mankind.

Marie Kerner, whispered loudly, "Here she comes," to get Judy Wisnewski and Judy Hart's attention away from Orlando North's good looks. Drape wondered if Lucille Cohen and Gladys Jacobsen still thought of Salvatore Bianco as a handsome man, as they had at her wedding shower. Jake Carrington was holding Professor Hazard's hand. Mr. and Mrs. Henderson were talking to Amanda Jenkins before she pointed to Drape's entrance. Jim Henderson clapped his hands, until his wife pulled his arm. Across the aisle, Mrs. Mack, Grandma, and Mother all turned to smile at her as she passed by.

Drape fixed her eyes on Sky, who seemed enthralled by all the silk and lace covering her. "It's me," she said after she'd let go of Professor Chinich's arm and mounted the step to stand by his side.

"I'm glad," Sky said.

Pastor Nieman took both their hands and began the ceremony. "We are gathered here in sight of God and this company ..."

* * *

Wedding Reception
Gandy Dancer Restaurant

Mother Taylor was arguing with Grandma as Sky and Drape entered the foyer. They stopped talking but whatever was bothering them hung in the air.

"Don't they have our reservations?" Drape asked, clearly reading their moods.

"Everything is fine," Grandma said.

"No it isn't," Mother Taylor insisted. "I don't expect her to take my advice or lean on Shakespeare's wisdom against King Lear's intentions 'to shake all cares and business from our years.' Your grandmother has decided to hand over half of her fortune to you two."

"Grandma," Drape scolded. "Wait until we come back from Hawaii."

"No," Grandma said. "Sky has been a saint about the way you were acting and I want to reward him."

Sky laughed with relief. "Grandma," he let go of Drape's hand long enough to embrace her. "Drape is all I'll ever need."

Larry Combs came in the door behind them. "I can't get the police to continue their surveillance. They say the wedding was accomplished, and they think Salvatore will forget about us now."

Burress was right behind him. "I checked with the police. The gunfire we heard did involve Bianco."

Sky realized Drape couldn't ask if Salvatore had been injured, because her new husband would have gotten upset.

"He escaped again?" Combs asked.

Drape laughed in relief. "My husband loves me. What can he do?"

The wedding guests had assembled in the main dining room past the lavish buffet. The band was already playing.

Professor Chinich came out into the foyer. He offered his hand to Grandma. "May I have this dance?"

"We have to wait for the bride and groom to dance," Grandma said.

"No we don't," Chinich said. "They have their whole lives. We only have a couple of decades left." With that, he dragged Grandma to the dance floor past the dining room. Sky caught a glimpse of them dancing the foxtrot to an eighties disco song.

The restaurant tables were covered in lace and the decorations from the church had been reassembled, draping the floor-to-ceiling windows facing the train tracks.

Drape clapped her hands. "Isn't it lovely, Sky?"

"You are," he said. And then the life seemed to drain out of him. He fell to his knees.

Salvatore Bianco appeared out of nowhere, behind Drape, holding a gun to her head.

* * *

Drape didn't know Salvatore was behind her for a second. She reached for Sky, who had collapsed on his knees. Then she heard Salvatore's voice.

"Too late for prayers, Sky." Salvatore grabbed Drape's arm and pulled her toward the windowed wall.

Drape saw the gun, but didn't believe Salvatore would use it.

Salvatore waved it at her guests. His hair was black now, black as his soul.

"No," she pleaded. "Salvatore, don't hurt my family."

"I won't," he said. "Come with me."

As if she thought she would never see them alive again, Drape refused to look away from her relatives. Mother Taylor had a steak knife in her raised arm. Grandma and Chinich were trying to help Sky up from his knees. Larry Combs was on his cell phone, hopefully calling for backup. Burress advanced toward them. Drape held up her hand for him to stop, and he did, pushing Ike behind him.

Salvatore yanked Drape through a narrow glass door to the patio outside.

Drape's skirt caught and ripped on the doorframe, delaying their exit. "Salvatore, stop," she cried. "I can't go with you."

"But you love me!" Bianco kept hold of Drape's hand as he shoved a bench in front of the door before pulling her toward the railroad tracks. "We can catch the commuter train to Chicago."

Drape heard a train coming. She could also hear the restaurant clientele inside start their traditional clapping and cheering to drown out the sounds of the freight train.

The wind whipped off her wedding veil. As Drape reached up for it, her hand caught in her pearls, and the beads danced around them. The white organza veil floated toward the oncoming eastbound train.

Bianco tripped backward on the loose pearls, falling off the patio stones and releasing Drape's arm just as the train sped by, taking his bodily evilness with it.

Sky had broken the windowed door and rushed toward her, clasping her against his chest. "I prayed," he said, shaking with emotion. "I prayed, and the Lord saved you!"

"And you were saved," Drape whispered, her heart nearly breaking with gratitude for the Lord's deliverance.

The End

Printed in the United States
By Bookmasters